Melody of Malice:

A Mississippi Mojo Thriller Series

Mary S. Palmer

&

Paula Lenor Webb

Mary S. Palmer & Paula Lenor Webb

An Intellect Publishing Book

Copyright 2023 Mary S. Palmer & Paula Lenor Webb

ISBN: 978-1-954693-96-8

Front cover design by Abe Partridge
Songs by Mike Turner and Mary S. Palmer

First Edition: 2023

FV-4

Visit the website: www.MississippiMurderBook.com

Intellect Publishing, LLC
6581 County Road 32, Suite 1744
Point Clear, AL 36564
www.IntellectPublishing.com

Dedication

Mary S. Palmer

To my outspoken aunt—Anna. She had red hair, but a heart of gold.

Paula Lenor Webb

My father, William C. Webb, who always supported my adventures!

Mary S. Palmer & Paula Lenor Webb

Acknowledgements

Abe Partridge

Shannon S. Brown

Muriel Nero

Mary Duffy

Mike Turner

Abe Partridge, who stuck it out with us in creating the Cover Art.

Mike Turner also partnered with Mary S. Palmer to write the songs recorded and in this book.

Mary S. Palmer & Paula Lenor Webb

Theirs not to reason why,
Theirs but to do and die…
Alfred, Lord Tennyson

Prologue

Deputy Zita Rocconi found her way to Mama Cheche's old home and sat in one of the rockers on the new front porch. It replaced the old porch ripped off by a tornado last year. It had taken a while and cost quite a bit, but now, the house, a Delta landmark, was returned to its original state. In fact, it was in better shape than it had been for years.

It was a cold March morning, but the police-issued jacket, wool pants, and boots kept the deputy warm. She rocked back and forth, across the newly planked floorboards, but it wasn't the same. She missed the rhythmic creaking sound the rocker used to make as she shared her thoughts and feelings with Mama Cheche. Zita wished the old lady were here now, because she wasn't sure what her next move should be. Mama would know. She had the Mojo.

It was surprising how Sheriff Hunter Harley, Shannon Brown, and her two children brought so much change in a short time to the small Delta town of Cleveland, Mississippi. Shannon had taken good care of Charles, her half-brother, and Karla, her half-sister left in her charge. Glancing down towards the Sunflower River, Zita saw the Tollar Plantation House and the cotton bin off in the distance to her left. No car was there, so she surmised that Shannon and the kids were not home when she drove by the house. *Probably taking the kids to school,* she thought.

She wasn't sure how things were going to turn out when Rapier Fogg, aka the Dallas Devil, had come to town and attempted to kill not only Charles and Karla, but Hunter as well. When Hunter's life was in danger, it scared her far more than she let anyone know. If she lost him, then she would lose a piece of herself. Before he came to Cleveland things were normal, well, her version of normal.

Zita liked getting up every morning in the small apartment behind her family home. Most days, she had a cinnamon roll and coffee for breakfast, and then headed off to work at the station. She also volunteered with Catholic Social Services, cooking food for the needy on holidays and delivering it. She drove older parishioners to doctors' appointments and enjoyed the stories they shared. She enjoyed doing all those things, but often wondered what it would be like to have someone do them with her. Like Hunter. He invited her to parties and was the type of man who didn't mind giving her a hand in personal matters, but he maintained a certain distance, a professional stance. She longed for more. *I wish he would hold my hand.*

Thinking of finding love, she then glanced towards the three headstones on a small rise to her right and her mood became somber. There stood the graves of Shannon's grandmother Eleanor, her mother, Ellie, and the grave of Goldie…but not quite. Rapier Fogg stole the urn with Goldie's ashes during the memorial ceremony. She died before telling where she'd put it. The entire police force was still keeping an eye out for its hiding place, but no luck so far.

Goldie and Eleanor sacrificed everything for love. They professed their love for each other, but it didn't work out. What if she told Hunter how she felt, would he give up his position as Sheriff in Cleveland and take off? Worse yet, what if she didn't share her feelings and kept it to herself? Then he and Shannon might start dating and get married.

Zita didn't have anything against Shannon, but she was a threat to other women. Men tended to be attracted to her confidence and take-charge attitude. She and Hunter were eating lunch at the Delta Dinner the other day and when Shannon walked into the room; she noticed how all the men suddenly sat up straight and glanced towards her. It was hard to compete with that.

Oh, Mama, I wish you were here. Zita thought, *You know how to handle things. You have the mojo, with its supernatural power. You also sacrificed a lot and took chances. It looks like I am going to have to do the same.*

Melody of Malice:

A Mississippi Mojo Thriller Series

Mary S. Palmer & Paula Lenor Webb

Chapter 1

Cleveland, Mississippi was astir. Excitement filled the air. This small town seemed distant from the rest of the world, but those who lived in it knew differently. It was growing into a tourist destination. Delta State University, home of the unusual Fighting Okra mascot, attracted college students for years, but now they had the Grammy Museum Mississippi, the Bologna Performing Arts Center, and the internationally known Tollar Plantation Cotton Bin Porch - where blues music was born.

Also, a new event had been added to Cleveland's attractions. Churches in town partnered with the Chamber of Commerce to hold an Easter Parade; a first for Cleveland and another sign of change. Zita stood on the front steps of the police station, watching the children excited to see the large white Easter Bunny riding on the back of a classic car through the center of town. She even caught a sweet whiff of cotton candy as a vendor handed the puff of pink to a child.

Everyone was in a festive mood, small brightly painted floats belted out peppy tunes as they drove down Main street, and the Delta State University Band played the school football fight song. She thought she saw Shannon's flaming red hair in the crowd, which meant Charles and Karla were here as well.

The first three months of the year had been uneventful as far as crime went, but this wasn't unusual. In the coldest time of year, it was best to stay off the icy roads. Now, even though it was chilly in early April, people were ready to stop being cooped up and have some fun. Half the town's 15,000 residents showed up for the event.

V, the antique store owner and Hunter's landlord who occupied the bottom floor of the building, was out in his front yard blowing leaves into the street early that morning when Zita passed by on her way to the station. His Cuban cigar—he only smoked the best—dangled from his lips as it dropped ashes on his white-streaked beard. Dressed in cutoff shorts and a white tank top, he danced to a peppy tune blasting through his iPod.

As Zita stood at her post in front of the Sheriff's office, she watched the patch of red hair move through the crowd and across the street. It was indeed Shannon Brown edging as close as she could get to Sheriff Hunter Harley, who stood watch in the same area.

Shannon had no claim on Hunter Harley. Zita sighed. *Neither do I.* She smiled, reminding herself that she and Hunter worked together and saw each other daily. Zita knew him better than Shannon and was around him at his worst and as his best. She knew first-hand that a sheriff's job wasn't easy. She admired and accepted all sides of Hunter, especially his tenacity. She tolerated him when he was down and tried to hide it. She wasn't sure Shannon could do that.

A recent change improved Hunter's mood dramatically, when his arrogant, know-it-all, but inefficient deputy, Carlton Newman, had another job arranged for him in Alabama. No one in the office cared why he left; they were all relieved he was gone.

When Hunter received a job application from a Harvard graduate, the first black man to win the Collins Cold Case Award in their Criminal Justice program, he wasted no time inviting that man to Cleveland for an interview.

Hunter and Zita were curious as to why Daryl Felder applied for a job in Cleveland when they both knew he could get a job anywhere he chose. They suggested as much when he was interviewed, but he hedged around and did not give an answer. They gave him a tour of the town, a synopsis of what his job might entail, and possible places to live, including the Shackem' Up Inn. Despite all of that, he still wanted the job, and they could not turn him down since his application was so strong.

It was obvious to Zita that Daryl did not need to prove himself when he strolled into the office on his first day of work. She arranged a place to stay, like she did with Hunter when he first moved into town. It did bother her a bit that Daryl Felder seemed to cozy up to her in a way. He had the habit of walking into her office and sitting down and stretching out his long legs even when she was clearly working on a case.

She respected him but wasn't interested in that way. Whether his attraction to her was imagined, or real, she wasn't sure. Maybe he was just a friendly type of person. He did get along with everyone and never acted superior, despite his esteemed background. She shrugged. *Time will tell and I'll deal with it, if or when I need to.*

A bump from the front brought Zita back to reality as she glanced down at a small boy at her feet. The boy's mother picked him up and said, "Sorry Bobby ran into you, Deputy. He's just excited." Zita nodded, as they rushed by and she glanced over the crowd again.

The Cleveland High School Band came around the corner blasting out the old favorite, *Easter Parade.* Their neatly pressed uniforms made them look classy. To Zita's dismay, though, they had crooked lines and didn't keep in step. The crowd didn't notice. Kids scrambled for candy thrown from the floats in all directions. Even adults picked up throws they'd never use and didn't want. Most handed over their loot to their children or grandchildren. Such insignificant trinkets were valued as much as gold, especially the stuffed bunny rabbits. They'd be taken home to be placed on a shelf and bragged about until next year.

As the last classic car, a 1958 Buick Limited, passed with Ms. Delta State riding and waving from the open top; Ms. Cleveland High School and others in it threw stuffed animals which were sought after the most. Even Zita caught a multi-colored stuffed egg which she promptly handed to a little girl who'd caught nothing. The fire engine followed with its lights whirling and horns blazing, signaling the end of the parade. She saw Shannon again with Charles and Karla in tow, but this time she was headed in Zita's direction.

"Hi! What a great parade!" said Shannon to Zita. "Are you going to be in the office in about an hour? I need to get the kids lunch, but I can come back in a little while. I have something to tell you. It's important."

"Sure," said Zita, but Shannon had already passed her and directed the kids to the new restaurant two doors down from the office. *So much for heading home for lunch.*

True to her word, Shannon arrived one hour later and took a seat in Zita's office. Zita noted her appearance. Her skirt to her ankles accentuated her slender figure and her blouse with a large red rose in the top center matched the skirt. It looked like a designer brand. Hunter had texted her earlier. He went home since he worked the night shift yesterday. Zita was glad Hunter had left for the day. She pointed to a chair and asked, "Where are the kids, Shannon?"

"Oh, I asked your new deputy to entertain them while we talked. It's the first time I've had a chance to meet him. He happened to be in the restaurant. We invited him to have lunch with us and he told them an Easter story, ha, ha. He's sure good-looking, isn't he? He appears to be great with kids, too. Said he would stay with them till we are finished."

"His name is Daryl…"

Shannon cut her off. "I read his badge. Daryl P. Felder, right? What's the *P* stand for? He is also sharp looking. He must iron everything or get it dry cleaned."

Hmm, maybe I can switch Shannon's attention to Daryl. Zita whispered, "He never said what the *P* stands for. Avoids it when it's brought up, so I guess it's a name he doesn't like. We were surprised when his resume said he was a Harvard graduate. He really wanted this job, and he is overqualified, but we could not turn him down. So far he is doing a great job."

The response she expected didn't come. Instead, Shannon shrugged. "Well, no matter what he's got, he can never measure up to Hunter."

Zita bit her tongue. "Okay. Now what's so important that you want to talk to me about?"

Steepling her index fingers, Shannon said, "You're not going to like this, but the kids' mother is on another rampage. I was informed Frederica is drinking and using drugs. "

"Who told you?"

"I'm not at liberty to say. As a lawyer, I can't repeat what my client tells me in confidence. But take my word for it, this is a reliable source. Frederica is trying to cause trouble again. Every time that happens, she says she wants the kids back and starts asking me for money and threatening me. It's extortion. You can bet she's dangerous."

"Is she in Cleveland? We thought she left town." said Zita.

"I don't know–yet." Shannon said. "Look, maybe I shouldn't have come. I'm just trying to prevent any trouble by giving you a heads-up."

"Shannon, you know it is to your benefit to let us know when she is in town. If you do not give us all the information, we might not be able to help you," said Zita in a serious tone.

Shannon stood, slung her purse strap over her shoulder, and turned to leave, indicating the conversation was over. Then she stopped. "Is Hunter here? I might do better talking to him."

Zita beat her to the office door and opened it. "Hunter's gone for the day. I'll relay this information to him." Without a word, Shannon walked out of the office and towards the restaurant to get her children.

Zita eased the door shut and went back to her office. *What else is going to happen today?*

Not five minutes later, Daryl walked into the office and sat in the same chair Shannon vacated. "That bombshell, Shannon, doesn't waste any time, does she?" He let out his breath. "She doesn't even observe the European distance between people talking. Man! When she picked up her kids, she got so close I thought she was going to step on my toes."

Zita chuckled. "Well, what does a good-looking guy like you expect?"

If he blushed, she couldn't tell because of his dark skin. He did give a quick retort. "Looks like she'd at least check to see if guys she's hitting on are married. Or, maybe that doesn't matter." He cocked his head. "I have seen her type before, but in big cities, not small towns. What is she doing here?"

Funny, Zita thought, *I could ask the same of you.* She kept quiet but continued to inform Daryl of a bit of town history. "Long story short, Shannon is the great-granddaughter of the famous Goldie Parsons. She inherited the Tollar plantation from her mother who had run off and married the black blues singer."

Daryl readjusted his position in his chair and then replied, "Oh, yeah! His body washed up from the Sunflower River decades later, not long after Hunter became sheriff, right?"

"Right. He solved the case, but it took a while," said Zita.

Then Zita's cell phone rang, she looked down at the screen to see it was Hunter calling her. "Daryl," she said, "It's Hunter. I am going to put it on speaker."

"Hi, Hunter, how is it going? I also have Daryl here." she said.

"Yea, he needs to be updated on this," said Hunter, "I just had the strangest call from Shannon. She said she had information Frederica is starting to cause trouble again. She also told me about talking to you and how you were not helpful, whatever that means. Excuse me, 'King, get out of that bowl!' Sorry, let me continue. Then she hinted that I should come to her house, but she didn't give any details on how she knew Frederica was around. You think she's overreacting?"

Zita looked up at Daryl, and whispered, "Probably." She cracked a smile when he shook his head. He probably didn't want to sound unconcerned. Shannon was right about one thing: Frederica could potentially be dangerous.

Hunter continued, "Okay, I'll let it ride for now. Frederica's no threat yet. We'll just stay on guard. I don't see anything else we can do. Keep Daryl informed. Thanks. Excuse me, 'King, stop chewing on the cord!' I got to go. See you tomorrow. Bye."

Zita put her phone back in her pocket as Daryl shrugged and stood to leave. "That cat is something! I've got to get back to work on *real* cases. I swear, I chose Cleveland expecting peace and quiet. Like Hunter, I didn't know a small town could have so much crime. Glad most of it is petty, but even those cases require written reports." He wiggled fingers on both hands. "Back to the keyboard." Then he winked, saying, "Bye, beautiful," as he walked out.

Zita wasn't comfortable with the compliment. She'd rather he'd turned his attention to Shannon, even though she knew that wasn't going anywhere. Shannon just liked to flirt.

Zita forced herself to think Daryl was just being nice, maybe he didn't mean anything more than that. She couldn't hold onto that thought. It nagged at her that maybe he wasn't. She also had another concern. Did Daryl really come to Cleveland for the reason he said? Or did he have an ulterior motive. Maybe her inquisitive mind was too busy.

She had work to do, too, so she put that thought aside as she scanned the latest files on her computer, looking for the most pressing case to start on.

Zita couldn't help but think about Mama Cheche again, she just knew Mama was the only person who could make sense of all of this.

"Hey, I am going to run to the courthouse; be back in an hour." Daryl opened the front door to the office and walked out. It caused a gust of wind to push through her office, blowing an older stack of printed case files onto the floor.

Zita sighed as she bent over to gather them all together. *Yes, one of those days.* The papers were bits of older cases she processed when the work was slow. A few of them were passed on to her when Carlton left. She bent over to pick up one sheet in the middle of the scattered pile, but it slipped from her hands. When she looked at it again, she saw a date from a couple of months ago scribbled on the top. Then, with another glance, what was written underneath caused her to gasp.

Chapter 2

The writing on the old piece of paper didn't relate to any case she knew about. Scrawled with dark gray pencil marks in the middle of the yellowed page in large, capital letters were the words *BOTTLE TREE.* *What the hell does this mean? What evil spirits can it ward off to serve its purpose? And how the hell did this sheet of paper get mixed in this stack?*

She held the paper up to her office light but didn't see a watermark bleed through. It had a distinct crease from being folded in half; it had been wet at some point and pressed against a newspaper. She saw black remnants on the paper with words in newspaper type. *Strange,* she thought, *I do not have a newspaper in my old files.*

To avoid damaging the fragile document further, she slipped on a plastic glove. Then she put the paper into a plastic sleeve she used to preserve evidence.

Next, Zita picked up the rest of the pages and files from the ground, glancing through them, looking at the folder she thought was before the old page and the one after. The piece of paper didn't seem to go with anything in the sack. The reports were about domestic occurrences with a husband and wife that repeated themselves anytime the husband had too much to drink--about once a month. Zita tried to help the wife, but she refused to press charges. It was an unending mess.

Zita knew this couple, like many others in town, did have a bottle tree in their front yard, but it was nothing special. She could not make a connection regarding the old piece of paper. In fact, she looked up the most recent call to their house, it was about the same time as the date written on the sheet. *Maybe Carlton added this to the top.*

Zita tried to visualize that particular bottle tree. She thought it was from the limb of a red oak. It held old and new beer bottles of different brands and colors–green, red, and blue–stuck on shaved down branches. It was placed right beside their rickety, wooden front porch steps. The corner of Zita's lip curled. That bottle tree may have done its job of keeping some spooks away from that house, but it sure didn't keep the demon of alcohol from causing problems. But how did their folder get on her desk? Tomorrow, she'd ask Hunter if he had put it there.

The next morning, Hunter and Zita had their usual confab over a cup of coffee in his office. This was a time she enjoyed because they discussed business, but personal interests often seeped into the conversation. Zita started their daily planning meeting by pulling out the piece of paper she'd found the day before and holding it up. "What do you know about this?"

Her question evoked a chuckle. Hunter recognized it immediately and said, "Carlton tried to make a big deal over that. I told him it was nothing and to toss it. Looks like he didn't. Where'd you find it?"

Hunter's cat, King, was visiting the office today and strutted out from under his desk. The cat got a pet from Zita as he rubbed against her ankles. Then he walked to his bowl and ate his breakfast.

Zita returned to the conversation. "I found it mixed in with the Falzoni case. Both were about the same date. I was going to get it checked for fingerprints."

"Carlton said he put that date on it. He already had it checked and found no prints but his own." Hunter waved his hand. "No need to waste time on it. Might as well throw it away." He pointed to the trashcan in his office.

Zita wasn't so sure he was right. She had an instinct and she wanted to pursue it. She didn't reply but silently vowed to see what she could find out before giving up on this piece of paper with BOTTLE TREE written on it. "I will take care of it," she told Hunter.

Hunter was distracted when his office phone rang and that was her cue to leave, King followed her. Back in her office, Zita slipped the paper right back where she found it as King hopped up on her desk. She scratched

King's head as her brain whirled with ideas of where to start her quest.

Trying to sort out her thoughts, she told King, "Two places come to mind when I think of bottle trees and where unfortunate things always seem to happen in this town. Mama Cheche's and the Tollar Plantation. They both have old bottle trees, I have seen them there all my life. Mama's tree is hidden in a wooded area behind her house; she showed me where it was years ago. The other one, on the Tollar Plantation, stands behind the cotton bin. She cringed. *And I'll have to go through Shannon to get to them. Hmm. Maybe not. I could sneak around when I know she's not home.* "What do you think, King?" Zita smiled when King meowed in agreement and rested his paw on the note.

"You know, cat, sometimes I think you are almost human." Zita scratched him behind the ear.

*   *   *

Zita knew Hunter's schedule for the day and when he left to patrol that afternoon, she used it as her moment to leave. It was also around the time Shannon picked up the children from school. She waited five minutes, left Daryl in charge of the office, and drove out to Mama Cheche's house and the Tollar Plantation.

First, she went to Mama Cheche's, driving by the Tollar place, hoping Shannon and the kids would not be there. She was right; nobody was anywhere around. She parked in front of Mama's house and walked to the woods behind the house, where the bottle tree was the last time she saw it. She pushed brush and branches aside, working her way to a small spot of high ground most did not know about.

There the old bottle tree stood. It had remained standing so long because the skeleton was built of old rebar, welded and twisted into a rough tree shape. Then the age of the tree was confirmed by the multicolored bottle that rested on its limbs. Canning jars from the early 1900s, early Coke bottles, small white cold cream bottles rested on short spikes, and an arrangement of blue, green, and yellow medicinal bottles were in the mix.

Zita took her time, shining the light from her iPhone through every bottle on the tree. If one looked like it had something in it she dusted it off so as not to miss anything. Halfway through a brown Coke bottle appeared to have something in it. It was on the tree upside down, so whatever was in there seemed intact. She slowly removed it from the tree and looked inside.

Yes! She exclaimed; *something was inside! Mama, did you put this here years ago? You clever lady! Who else could have?*

Zita then heard a rustle in the leaves by her feet. A snake? A rat? She wasn't taking chances and she'd found what she was looking for. She slipped the bottle into her jacket pocket and made her way back through the woods to her patrol car. There was still the bottle tree at Shannon's house, but it was getting time for her to come back home and for Hunter to return. *I'll keep my secret. No point in bringing this up at this stage of the game.* Zita thought.

She paused for a moment remembering the plans made for this place. She hoped one day it would be a museum for Goldie. But it didn't look like that would happen soon. From scuttlebutt, it seemed Shannon couldn't proceed with the project because she didn't have the money. The cost to repair the Tollar Plantation house and Mama's home was more than she expected. Remodeling it into museum prices were prohibitive and then there was Charles and Karla to consider. Shannon had savings, but she'd had to dip into them to survive. An attorney in this small town didn't have a lucrative income.

Zita did give Shannon credit. She was dedicated to restoring the history of this property. In this venture, Zita hoped Shannon would find a way to make her dream come true. As Cleveland's most famous blues singer, Goldie never lived to see it, but he deserved the honor.

In another situation, Zita withheld good wishes for Shannon. When it came to dealings with Hunter, Zita vowed to do her best to squash any overtures put forth by her rival. As far as Hunter was concerned, Shannon was off limits. How she could enforce those limits, Zita hadn't figured out. But she knew one thing: she'd do whatever it took.

Zita returned to the office and walked in the door in time to hear him calling out "Hell" and "Damn", the strongest curse words he ever used; she knew he was upset.

"What's the problem, Boss?" Zita asked as she entered his office. King was not in sight; Hunter must have taken him back home.

For a moment, he glared at her. "Carlton," he sneered. "Wouldn't you know it? I got another call from Shannon. She's getting phone calls from random numbers and they hang up when she picks up the phone. She acts calm, but I know she's frightened, for herself and the children. She left their house and went out to eat an early supper. Damn it all; it's bound to be Frederica." He slammed his fist on his desk. "I can't find Frederica's file on my computer and Shannon is holding back information! Maybe I can use something in the file. What the hell could Carlton have done with it? Did he save it? Or delete it? He doesn't answer his damn phone, either." Punctuating each word with a shake of his fist, he added, "I could wring his neck."

Zita held up both palms. "Just calm down. I can tell how upset you are when you start cursing…"

He swung around. "I don't curse; I only swear. You know why? I'll tell you. Maybe it'll get my mind off of that dumb jerk for a minute." He plopped into his chair and Zita sat opposite him in front of his desk.

"First of all, if my mother heard me use profanity, she'd have made sure I couldn't sit down for a week. My dad taught me a lesson about expressing my anger with other bad words." He cut his eyes to the ceiling. "When I was thirteen years-old, I stood up to my dad one day after he refused to teach me to drive like my friends were doing. I spewed out every vulgarity I'd ever heard."

He cracked a smile. "To my surprise, my dad didn't give me a smack or even yell at me. He calmly sat me down and had me write each word on a piece of paper. Then he handed me a dictionary and told me to define each one. I looked at him like he was crazy, but I did as he said." He looked at Zita as he shook his finger in her face. "You know what? Even a teenager could see none of them made sense. Dad made a profound statement, one I'll always remember. 'Son, he said, 'Cursing is the effort of a feeble mind to express itself.'

"Dad didn't have to explain that those words were spouted out for shock value." He guffawed. "They may have been shocking then, but nobody's shocked with anything nowadays. So," he stood, "using them is an exercise in futility. I've never used them since—hell and damn are strong enough words to vent my anger."

Zita laughed aloud. "I'm not laughing at you. It's the concept. It's nutty but your dad, and you, are right. Come to think of it, those words *are* meaningless. Your dad was a smart man." She stood. "Okay, give me Carlton's office number and I'll catch up with him. If Frederica's starting trouble, we'll nip it in the bud, but I have to say I am not crazy about Shannon using client confidentiality as a reason to hold stuff back from us."

Zita looked up the number in her office, but she didn't use it. She had something better. She took out her own phone and pushed the buttons to Carlton's cell phone. With a smile, she heard a male voice respond on the third ring.

"Is that you, Zita? What's up? Y'all must need my help." said Carlton.

His indirect bragging turned her off, but she had to go with it. She got right to the point without amenities. "Yes, we do. Hunter is looking for the file on Frederica and it's not where it should be. We know you organized everything in the office. Do you remember where you entered it on the computer? We can't..."

Carlton didn't let her finish the sentence. "It IS where it should be, I saved it, probably under 'Frederica' and I printed out most of it to read and put that folder in the third drawer of the file cabinet with closed cases. What's going on with that woman now?"

Zita withheld a sigh. She didn't tell him anything more than, "Oh, this is just a routine check." Then a light flashed in her brain. "I do have another question for you..."

"Shoot. I can answer it."

"Did you put the old piece of paper on my desk with the words BOTTLE TREE printed on it? I found it next to the Falzoni file. If so, it's okay. I just want to follow up on it." She rubbed her finger over the top of the brownish Coke bottle sticking out of the pocket of the jacket she was still wearing.

He hesitated, causing Zita to wonder if he knew something he wouldn't tell her. Then, he stammered out, "I, er, I, no, I didn't. I would've remembered, I'm sure. Well…but Hunter made me stop. He said to quit wasting time on it…the note. Say, have you discovered something?"

Zita wasn't going to tell him what she knew at this point. "No, Carlton, I haven't. I just saw the paper and asked Hunter about it."

"If you do find it's important, please let me know. I still think it has some significance. My office phone's ringing. Gotta catch it. Bye."

"Damn! No luck about the note with Carlton!" Standing, Zita jerked off her jacket and rested the old Coke bottle on her desk.

Chapter 3

The Coca-Cola bottle Zita picked up after putting on a pair of plastic gloves was nothing like any she'd seen before. It was amber-colored with a diamond-shaped label. She had read about those and recalled that it was done to make it stand out more, and it had worked. It dated back to 1907. Her gloves kept her from making fingerprints in the dust covering the straight-sided bottle as she turned it from one side to the other. *How many hands had this bottle been held by? How did it survive over a century? Was it valuable?*

She shined the light from her iPhone through it once more. A piece of rolled paper was tucked into the bottom, kept safe from the elements all these years. Her heart raced. How was she going to get it out without tearing it? Her only option was to break the bottle. She made sure no one saw her as she slipped outside. They didn't; Hunter's door was closed and Daryl was nowhere in sight.

As she eased out the back door of the office into the alley, she banged the bottle on the concrete, shattering it to pieces. She picked the note out from amongst the shards, gathered up the debris, and put it into a plastic grocery bag she'd brought along for that purpose. Her fingers shook as she unfolded the yellowed paper very carefully. Then she read the brief words written in a scrawling handwriting:

My WIFE,

I miss you so much and I hope we will be together soon, but I've got to be careful. We can't trust old Wylie. This song's in my head, but I don't want him to steal it. He'll never look in any bottle tree for it. Cheche, and now you since you must have figured out the BOTTLE TREE message, are the only ones I told it was here. My hope was that you'd remember the R C Cola we shared on our way to Memphis and make the connection to this Coke bottle. If you're reading this, maybe it worked. Anyhow, Wylie would have a problem trying to claim the song; I know the music and he doesn't. Here are the lyrics I've written so far:

There's things comin' round

And it's all bad news

I'm 'bout to drown

And it gives me the blues.

Bad News Blues

Just read the headlines.

I'm in o'er my head,

And it sure is a crime.

Bad News Blues.

Oh! I'm a-hurtin'

Got a dark, dread feelin'.

One thing is certain

Bad News Blues got me reelin'.

Bad News Blues

And though how I try

There ain't no escapin'

Feel the end's comin' nigh.

Bad News Blues.

Oh, Lord. I've got to get the other 3 verses on paper. I have to go now. Wylie is waiting on me. Later, I'll write down the rest of the lyrics for you and hide them, too. Oh, Eleanor, I hope you find these someday, even if I'm gone.

All my love,

Goldie

Tears filled Zita's eyes. *Poor Goldie, and poor Eleanor. They had so little time together. Sad, and so unfair. Life is cruel. The song stays focused on Goldie, but real life is a melody of malice.*

Zita slipped the note into her shirt pocket and headed back inside. She put the bag with the bottle's broken pieces into the trash on her way. Taking out the note, she reread it. Before she had time to move it from her desk to a safe place, Daryl made one of his unannounced office visits.

Zita pulled off the plastic gloves and tossed them into the trash can.

"What's with the gloves?" Daryl pointed to her hands as he leaned forward. She moved the note aside. It fell to the floor and he picked it up. "What's this?"

She all but snatched the paper from his hands. "Oh, nothing really. I, er, was getting ready to check out Frederica's folder. Carlton told me where to look for it."

Daryl frowned. "You need gloves for that?"

"I might if I have to go to storage in the Court House, it's dusty in there. Sometimes something new shows up."

Daryl shrugged. "Okay. Let me know if it does. That's a strange case. Oh, by the way, I'm kind of curious about your most famous case, Goldie Parsons. People here sure like to rehash that one. Where would I find those old records?"

Zita noticed Daryl's body language changed with that statement. The once relaxed posture of the man stiffened as he pulled his legs in and leaned in closer to her, sitting on the edge of the chair. Features of his face tightened and his gray eyes became serious. *Interesting.* She thought.

Zita pretended not to notice as she tried to keep her voice steady. The coincidence of Daryl bringing up

Goldie's case at this moment was uncanny. "They may have been moved to the Court House too, hence the gloves, but there should be a few in the back room under his name. It was all solved, you know."

"I know. But how it played out intrigues me. I enjoy learning about cold cases. Don't worry. I'll check it out on my own time. Right now. Bye, Babe."

Daryl hurried out of the room a little faster than normal, leaving Zita to wonder about him. She expected him to dig deeper into her unusual actions, to question the gloves, maybe even her motivation. Unless he didn't want his own motivation questioned. How would he have responded if she'd asked him *exactly* why he was interested in the Goldie Parsons case?

I'm probably just overreacting. I need to switch my thoughts to something else. Goldie had to be the last person to touch that bottle as he slipped his note into it. Zita took a deep breath. Goldie hinted there were more verses to the song. Did it have a title; if so, was it *Bad News Blues*? The morose choice of words and fatalistic attitude certainly fit the mold of the blues, sadness and suffering. In four lines, it expressed all the hopelessness of a doomed man.

She shook off a chill. Excitement invaded her bones. She couldn't wait to share this news. Zita frowned. But with whom? Not Shannon. *If the rest of the song is found and set to music, I know she would be the lawful heir. But it's premature to let her in on it now.* Nor would it be safe to confide in Hunter; he might tell Shannon. No need to give them reasons to be together, a common bond. Thoughts whirled in her brain.

Zita justified her secrecy by assuring herself that this find had no connection to any police matters. The Parsons' case was over and done with. The bottle find couldn't prove, or disprove, anything. *IF* she unearthed more lyrics to the song, *IF it was proved to be written by Goldie, and IF it was worth a fortune*, then she'd have plenty of time and reasons to turn it over to its rightful inheritor—Shannon Brown.

With the thought that such an inheritance could enable the Goldie Parsons' Museum to become a reality, Zita took the note out of her pocket and slipped it into an evidence bag and in the desk drawer where she kept office supplies, and she locked it. When her shift was over, she'd take it home for safekeeping.

As she worked on other pressing cases during the day, Zita's thoughts drifted to where the rest of the verses might be hidden–which escaped her imagination–to how Mama Cheche's house would look converted to a museum holding whatever artifacts of Goldie's they could acquire.

In her mind's eye, Zita pictured Goldie's guitar encased and hanging on a wall or under glass on a shelf, maybe along with a zoot suit, and perhaps his wedding photo. Zita got very little work done all day. She was too preoccupied with daydreaming and a tingle of fear. What if she never found any more bottles with verses or notes from Goldie? After more than half a century, anything might have damaged or destroyed the pieces of paper they were written on. She was lucky this one survived, but what about the others?

At home that evening, after eating a ham sandwich and a handful of chips. She took out the note, spread it out on her kitchen table, trying to press out the folds to get a better look. She also took out the BOTTLE TREE note and laid it next to the paper.

She reread the verses word by word, looking for symbols or hidden meanings. *I see Carlton's date on here, but why didn't Goldie at least put a date on this? How long was it before he died?*

Zita pulled out a small plastic ruler from the junk drawer and put it on top of the document. She rested it under the title, blocking the rest of the text since it was first. If it was *Bad News Blues,* it clearly meant Goldie knew something bad was about to happen. He'd borrowed Wylie's car to go to Memphis and get married. *Looks like it was written after he returned to Cleveland.* She glanced over at the other note and then back at the one in front of her, wishing she had a mojo stone like Shannon. She remembered what Mama Cheche used to say, *Mojo, do your stuff. Give me the answers.* If only she could invoke the Mojo herself!

Then Zita thought, *Goldie had to be here in Cleveland to hide this note in this bottle. So he put it there not long before he died.*

Ideas flitted through her brain. When and why did he lose trust in Wylie? Zita had read the old files, and she grew up hearing a lot of the local gossip. She had looked up the history of Wylie's music career and he'd followed the path of a man consumed with music, which brought fame and wealth.

Wylie opened each of his performances by telling everyone he sold his soul to the devil, so it was common knowledge. He also referred to Goldie in his shows, saying if he'd done the same thing, he probably wouldn't be missing. He must have resented Goldie putting his love for Eleanor first, so Zita wondered why he loaned Goldie his car to go to Memphis and get married.

Zita sat up in the chair a bit straighter, as it squeaked from the movement, she touched her forehead. *Wait a minute. Maybe he didn't. Shannon said Goldie didn't plan to take Eleanor off with him. Her grandmother said it all happened because of her domineering mother's actions. Goldie rescued her in the passion of the moment. Aha! Looks like he and Wylie had a breakup over that when Goldie returned Wylie's car.*

Zita cracked a smile. She knew she didn't qualify to have the mojo, but somehow it worked for her. She slid the ruler down to the first verse and the depth of its despair struck her. The second line of the next verse stopped her: *Just read the headlines. That has to be a clue. But what?* Eleanor was from a prominent family, and her debut could have made the headlines in the social section of the newspaper. But her mixed marriage sure didn't. Elma lied to keep anyone from knowing the truth. Zita rested her chin in the cup of her palm. *Newspapers, headlines. What does it refer to? Why can't I figure it out?*

She moved the ruler to underline the next two verses which seemed to express pain, suffering, and agonizing over a fate Goldie found inescapable. These verses covered it all. *What's left to say?*

Zita looked at the clock above the sink. It was almost midnight, and she was exhausted. She couldn't decipher anything else tonight. She slipped the paper back into the plastic bag and placed it high on a linen closet shelf behind stacks of sheets and towels. She was certain nobody would look for anything there. Then she headed to her bedroom and got ready for bed, maybe a good night's sleep would refresh her.

The last thought she had before falling asleep was: *I think the clue is in the one line I can't figure out. But how many newspaper headlines will I have to read to unearth what that damn clue means?* The magnanimity of the task kept her awake half an hour. Then sleepiness overcame her, and she gave in hoping the mystery wouldn't invade her dreams.

Chapter 4

Zita's dream was vivid with details from the past. She was sitting at her desk at the police station when she heard dance music from the forties filling the space. She wondered if Chan, who loved blues music, was messing with her. Then she realized her computer was missing and instead, stacked in front of her, were newspapers. The headlines in bold black letters read, U.S. AND JAPS AT WAR, BOMB HAWAII, PHILIPPINES, GUAM, SINGAPORE. She pushed the top part of the stack aside and read another alarming headline, PRESIDENT SIGNS DECLARATION OF WAR; 350 CASUALTIES AS JAPS BLAST MANILA.

What was going on? She wondered. Then she heard a tap, tap, tap of a shoe and looked up to see a blue-eyed man, dressed in a zoot suit, of all things, and wing tipped shoes. He grinned and it was as if her heart stopped - he flashed a gold tooth. *Goldie Parsons!*

Her alarm clock blasted at six a.m., and she jerked up fully awake, sheets tangled in her legs as she tried to get up to turn off the alarm. She slammed the button with more force than intended and rubbed her eyes.

There was more to the dream, but that was all she could remember. That dream meant something important. Zita believed things could be revealed in dreams, Jesus sometimes revealed himself in them, but did this one have any real significance? For now, she put it aside, untangled the sheets and made her bed. Then she showered and dressed for work in her uniform.

The scent of fresh coffee perking filled her small kitchen while Zita worked on a plan. As she poured some sweetener into her cup, she realized this was her secret and she'd have to research cautiously.

Daryl had asked about the files on Goldie's case, but Hunter placed him on patrol all day yesterday and he hadn't gotten them yet. As she sipped her coffee, she knew that would give her an excuse to pull them.

Stirring sweetener into her second cup of coffee, she tried to find a reason not to give all of them to Daryl so she could study them herself. But how could she justify parceling them out? *I can get to the office early, divide up the printed files, and make digital copies under different names. Then I'll say I only found one file or folder, and the others must be misfiled or deleted by accident. That should work.*

She ate one piece of wheat toast with homemade strawberry jam, savored the sweet taste, and dashed out the door. On the short trip to the office, she said a Hail

Mary asking that Daryl didn't beat her there this morning.

When she arrived, Hunter was at his desk, and God was on her side, Daryl had not arrived yet. She gave a sigh of relief and said to Hunter, "Morning, Boss. If you don't have anything pressing for me to do, Daryl asked me about the files on Goldie Parson's case. Is it okay if I look them up for him? It may take a while to locate them on the computer. Carlton said he printed some, but I seem to recall them being out of order."

"What's with Daryl and the case?" He raised an eyebrow. "Does he have anything new on the urn, by any chance?"

"I don't think so. He said he's just curious." Zita rubbed her chin. "Say, I think Daryl's from Mobile or, hmm, what's the name of that island down there? Not Dauphin Island, a smaller one."

"You mean Mon Louis Island? You may be right. I read his resume, but I didn't focus on anything beyond his college record at Harvard. He's one smart guy—graduated with high honors. It still confuses me why he wants to be here. Okay, go ahead and dig out those files and let Daryl study them. Maybe he's the brain we need to find out where that damn urn is located."

Zita left Hunter's office sporting a broad grin. Some greater good may come from Daryl's curiosity, something she hadn't thought of. It could lead to the urn, or it could help her analyze the meaning of the verses of that song on the old piece of paper. This could reap benefits for them all. She bypassed her office, walked to the back room, and switched on the light.

The evidence room was fairly orderly. Carlton claimed it was a mess. Hunter was willing to do anything to get him out of everyone's hair. So he let Carlton clean up the room and rearrange the layout. Hoping to find the files Carlton had printed to read, Zita opened one file cabinet and rummaged through the files in alphabetical order. Most of them contained physical evidence, but she still checked. The "P's" were in a cabinet on the top shelf, so she had to get the office ladder to reach them. On the second to the top shelf, she reached for a box of files and four came tumbling down, hitting the floor with a loud bang.

The tape on two boxes broke and random files spilled out. Zita scooped them up and looked at the box labels. One was "Parnell, John" and the other was "Parton, Edgar." Nothing in between, no "Parsons, Goldie." She stared at the shelf's blank space and at the boxes before and after, backing up to the "O's" and moving forward to the "Q's."

She put the files back into their boxes. *Good Lord, my plan turned out to be real. I'm going to have to go through all the boxes to find Goldie's. IF I can find it. How in the world did it really get misplaced? I don't even know what physical evidence box it is in. Shannon probably got Goldie's gold tooth, so it wouldn't be here. What else was there? I'd better check with Hunter to see if someone has it. Maybe Daryl came back and got it late yesterday.*

When Zita returned to Hunter's office, Daryl was there. She barged right in and asked, "Umm, Daryl, did you get those files on Goldie? I checked the evidence room and didn't find anything. I thought maybe you went to the courthouse storage to see if anything was there. "

To her dismay, he replied. "Haven't had a chance to go to either place. I was just going to look for them here. Why?"

Zita shook her head. "Don't bother. I went to get them for you and they're gone. At least they're not in place. I don't see anything about the case on the computer, either."

Hunter squinted. "Are you sure? Chan told me Carlton stored the old ones in the courthouse and the newly printed files here." He made two fists. "Oh, Lord, if Carlton had his hands on them, no telling where they are. I don't think that Dufus ever learned the alphabet."

Zita sniggered. Deputy Chan had been on the force in Cleveland before Hunter and he was efficient. But Carlton wasn't, so he could've put those files anywhere. "Well," she said, "He was creative in his filing system. I remember him saying he liked to file by first names because he could remember those better. Let me take another look. Maybe I can find them. I'd rather do that than call him. He'll take thirty minutes and tell me a couple of stories before he gets to the point. IF he ever gets to the point." She shrugged. "I'll send him an email later if I still can't find them. You know we can't depend on Carlton for any help. He doesn't have a good memory." With a wave, she left the room.

In the musty back room, Zita sneezed twice as she replaced the four boxes on the high shelf and took a second look at any nearby. None was labeled "Parsons" or "Goldie." She pulled a tissue from her back pocket and blew her nose and then continued searching until she'd moved the ladder five times and read labels on all of the boxes on that shelf. "Hells bells! No luck at all. How else could they be filed?" *Wait a minute.* She scratched her cheek. *Maybe he filed them by the date of the crime. Could he have possibly placed the new files with the old files in the courthouse storage? God, I'll have to look back sixty years in that dusty old room under the courthouse stairs. Those old files were never digitized. I may never find the recent ones on the computer if Carlton messed with those. Talk about a problem. This can really develop into one.*

After two hours of searching every box of folders with no results, Zita had to get some fresh air to stop her sneezing fits. She had accomplished one thing. She'd found Frederica's file where Carlton said it was. He'd printed out the entire file. She stopped by Hunter's office. Since he wasn't there, she left that folder on his desk. No need to try to explain why it was in the wrong folder. It wouldn't make sense.

Then Zita went back to her office, turned on her computer and spotted an email from Carlton: *Have you looked in the Falzoni Domestic folders? I was on call at their house and then met Chan at Mama Cheche's. Two workers were in a fight and we had to separate them. I just remembered they'd taken down some walls and newspapers that had covered holes were all over the floor. I picked up a sheet of paper with the words BOTTLE TREE on it and I must have stuck it in the Falzoni file. This happened not long before I left Cleveland. I didn't get a chance to investigate it, but it's probably unimportant. Look with the "F's" for Goldie's files. It may be in a box shoved behind Falzoni's. I did what I could, but that back room is still a mess.*

As usual, Carlton didn't take the blame. He offered no apologies, but just brushed off anything that happened to him as somebody else's fault. No matter, Zita was glad to discover where the paper about the Bottle Tree came from and to get a lead on where the Goldie's files may be. She dashed back to the file room to see if it paid off.

Chapter 5

Zita folded up the ladder and placed it in the corner since she didn't need it to reach the box labeled "F." Daryl came looking for her and was tall enough to reach the high shelf. Except for the Falzoni folder, the one containing the piece of paper that didn't belong, she saw a box marked with that name was in its rightful place.

"Daryl," said Zita. "Can you hand me that box?"

"Sure," he replied as he brought it down. "Wait, I see something. Take this so I can check behind it." He'd retrieved a folder that was pressed up against the back wall marked "Goldie Parsons, updates."

Zita and Daryl were both excited to discover what they were looking for until Daryl unwrapped the twine binding the folder together.

"Ah, man! It's empty! "Daryl tossed the folder to the ground. Zita, nothing's here." He stared at her, eyebrows pinched. "Got any other ideas?"

She tapped her fingers on a nearby shelf. "Not really. But we can recheck under 'Goldie', in case I missed something."

They followed along the shelf from the "F's" to the "G's"; still nothing.

"I just remembered one other place! Sheriff Gaines liked to keep the old files he pulled in the office instead of running them back to storage in the courthouse. They are in the old cabinet in the supply closet."

They opened the door to the supply room to be met with the smell of bleach, wet mops, and black mildew lingering in the corners. They pushed aside a mop bucket to find an old file cabinet hidden amongst the debris.

"Eureka!" said Zita as she opened the rusty file cabinet bearing folders and papers from years past. Halfway through she realized many of the files were not in alphabetical order.

"I'm appalled," Daryl said. "Who could be so inefficient?"

"Carlton!" Zita blurted out. "It looks like he filed some cases under last names, some under first ones, and others by date. All of them could've been digitized in the amount of time finding them took. What the hell was he thinking?"

She shook her head. "Oh, it's just Carlton, he *wasn't* thinking. That's the problem." She tapped her finger against her temple. "The only other place is the storage in the County Court House and that could take hours."

Daryl sighed, "I guess this is what we will have to do."

Zita nodded in agreement. Then she heard Hunter yelling, "Where are the two of you?"

Before she answered, he slammed the supply closed door against the wall, yelling, "Come on! We've got a call from the Tollar Plantation from Charles, but he was crying and not coherent. Let's get going before something terrible happens. It could be Frederica." He turned to Daryl. "Come in your car. You know the way. Zita, you ride with me."

Within seconds, they bolted out the office door, and were headed to the Tollar Plantation, sirens blaring. When they first pulled into the front yard, nothing seemed amiss.

As everyone got out of their cars, Zita paid attention as Hunter directed everyone where to go. "Zita, you take one side of the front door, I will take the other. Daryl, go around back in case someone comes out that way."

Pulling out their guns, they did as they were told.

Zita nodded at Hunter, indicating she was ready as she stood by the front door. He then yelled, "Shannon, it's Hunter."

They heard no answer.

Hunter knocked and called out again, louder this time. "Shannon, it's Hunter. Are you okay?"

Hunter pulled open the screen door and then opened the main door. He glanced at Zita as it opened easily when he pushed against it. She looked afraid of what they might find. Zita kept her pistol ready, providing cover, as he entered the foyer one step at a time. She moved in behind him taking small steps, looking towards the living room on the left, then the kitchen door in front of them. They cleared the space and Zita worked her way to the back door, letting Daryl in.

Daryl mouthed to Zita, "Where are they?"

She whispered back, "I don't know."

Hunter took the stairs two at a time. In a few minutes, he came back down. "No one's anywhere around. I'm baffled. It only took ten minutes to get here. Oh, God! I hope Frederica didn't kidnap all of them."

"We need to check to see if Shannon's car is here," Zita suggested.

"It's possible that they took her car. Everything is wide open. I wonder where the security cameras are. We need to check them." Hunter took out his phone and ordered an all-points bulletin, a *Be on the lookout.*

"That will only do some good IF the culprit is Frederica," Zita said.

Hunter nodded. "I know, but I have to do something." He stiffened his shoulders. "Let's take a look outside and in the cotton bin, I think that is where

Shannon parks her car. If it's not there, we need to get busy searching. Nothing in the house is disturbed, I find it unusual. Did either of you notice anything out of place?"

Zita and Daryl shook their heads.

Then Zita snapped her fingers. "Wait a minute." She walked towards the table in the foyer "Something is missing– there was a photo of the kids with Santa Claus here. See? Here is the dust outline from the frame."

"That's a clue. Maybe Frederica did pay a visit. She's the only one likely to take that photo." Hunter waved his hand toward her. "Let's see if her car is here."

They walked outside and pulled the door closed. Glancing towards the great oak tree where the car was usually parked made it clear the car was missing.

"Look, Boss, a car is coming. I think it's Shannon's," said Zita, spotting a dust cloud headed in their direction from the main road.

"Well, at least we know where they are," Hunter told Zita as Shannon's car drove up.

Shannon got out looking a little disheveled, not the perfect image she normally portrayed. She smoothed her hair, trying to tame bits of frizz. "Oh, I'm sorry Charles called you. It was a false alarm. I would've called you back, but I had to hurry to the bank."

Hunter stood with his hands on his hips. "To the bank? What was the rush?"

"I thought I was overdrawn." She didn't make eye contact with anyone.

Charles and Karla got out of the car and stood by their half-sister. They fidgeted around, glancing at each other and then at Shannon.

Charles spoke up. "I made a mistake. I'm sorry I called. I thought Karla had gone missing again, so I called you. But she, umm…was just upstairs."

Wide-eyed, Hunter looked at the three standing close together. "Okay, Charles, but why didn't you look upstairs before panicking?"

Charles looked at Shannon and she replied. "He was scared, and with just reason. His sister had been missing before, remember? Besides, you know how kids are, Hunter. They don't think like adults."

Zita didn't speak up, but she didn't see Charles, a precocious child, as overacting. *Nope. Charles was upset by more than they said. Something was wrong here. Terribly wrong.*

"Let's go inside and discuss this further. I need a little more information for my report."

Hunter sent Daryl back to the station and led the way. In the living room, Zita and Hunter remained standing, while Charles sat in the large stuffed chair. Shannon eased onto the sofa and pulled Karla next to her. Karla pulled up the sleeves of her pink top revealing a large bruise.

Zita moved close to Hunter and pointed out what she spotted. Hunter's eyes narrowed and in a tone he typically used to get information from criminals, he asked, "Karla, what happened to your arm?"

Karla's mouth fell wide open, but no words came out. She jerked the sleeves back down.

Shannon spoke up. "She banged a door against it. It's nothing serious."

"Which door?" asked Zita, certain they were lying.

Simultaneously, Karla and Shannon replied.

"The back door," Shannon said.

"The kitchen door," Karla replied.

Zita and Hunter glanced at each other and silently nodded at each other. Zita looked at the group. Shannon still did not make eye contact with anyone and Charles and Karla struggled not to squirm in their seats.

Hunter steepled his index fingers as he paced in the living room. "Um-hum. Now, Shannon, tell me what *really* happened." After a silent pause, he pointed in the direction of where the missing picture had been. "Where's the photo of the kids with Santa Claus?"

"I dropped it while dusting and the glass broke, so I put the photo away until I can get a new piece of glass."

"Okay, get it and show it to me."

"Oh, er, no, I didn't do that." She snapped her fingers. "Now I remember. The picture was damaged, so I threw it away. We can take a new one next year."

Zita rolled her eyes. *She's a fast thinker.*

Hunter was a step ahead of Shannon. "Okay, where's the empty frame?"

Shannon had a quick response for that, too. "It came apart. I tossed it, too."

Hunter came over and took Karla by the hand. "Let's go into the kitchen and you can show me just how you got that bruise, okay?"

When Shannon tried to follow, Hunter told her, "No, you stay here," and she did. He motioned Zita to follow him.

When they reached the kitchen and Karla couldn't tell him which door she'd bumped into she started sobbing. Zita put her arm around the child's shoulders. "Just tell us the truth and everything will be alright, Honey."

Blinking back tears, Karla said, "Shannon will be mad if I do."

"We'll take care of that. Don't you worry. Just tell us what happened."

Shannon burst into the room. "You can't question her without me present."

Hunter gave her a glare. Pointing a finger at her, he said. "Stand back. It will be smart of you to let Karla tell us the truth or you can do so."

Shannon sunk into a kitchen chair. She looked at Karla's tear-stained cheeks. "Okay. Leave Karla alone. I'll tell you what happened. But you've got to protect us." She took the Mojo stone from the center of the table and held it up. "I even resorted to putting my faith into this, but it didn't work. I can't fight anymore. I give in." She put down the stone and rested her head in cupped palms while tears flowed onto her own cheeks.

"At 8:30 this morning, after the kids had missed the school bus, I was rushing to drive them to school when I heard a knock at my door. It was Frederica who forced her way inside screaming that she wanted $10,000 or she'd take the kids right now. I do not know how she got past the cameras. Karla must have heard the noise and ran into the room. Her mama grabbed her arm and twisted it behind her back. Charles then ran in and saw what was happening. This was the phone call he made to you from the house phone. I knew we were too far outside of town to get help soon so I told Frederica I'd give her what I had in my checking account–about $3,000–to let Karla go, and she agreed."

"How did she get to your house?" Hunter asked.

Shannon shrugged. "I don't know; I didn't see a car, or anything. The cameras didn't make a sound letting me know someone was out there. She told Charles to put the phone down, stuffed that photo of the kids with Santa into her backpack, and then ordered everyone into my car. The bank just opened, so we drove up to the teller. She sat in back with Karla. I kept looking in the rearview mirror and it looked like she had something sharp against Karla's side. I wasn't going to risk letting the teller know something was wrong. I wrote a check for cash. They gave it to me, and then I drove away.

"She then told me to pull over behind that small grocery store about a mile outside town. She grabbed the money from my hand and then she threatened me again. 'I'll be back in a few days and you better have the rest of the money!' she said. "She shoved Karla, jumped out the car, and disappeared around the corner. I didn't see where she went. I hightailed it home."

Zita listened as Hunter probed for more information, but none was forthcoming. Reluctantly, she had to admit that Shannon showed true concern for the welfare of her half brother and sister. She put them before herself and that was admirable. But the culprit in this case was a danger to be reckoned with. Whether Shannon could protect her charges against a sociopath like Frederica remained to be seen. Even if she didn't like the situation, Zita had to do everything in her power to help Shannon keep her enemy at bay. Not only did her oath as an officer of the law require it, so did her moral values. She made another vow: *No matter what it takes, I'll do my job and follow my conscience, so help me God.* She swallowed hard. *But it isn't going to be easy. No, it's not!*

Chapter 6

Hunter promised to have his deputies keep a close watch on the Tollar Plantation until further notice. Shannon took precautions, too. She found out the cameras needed a software update to work. She made the updates along with a notation to check them more often. She drove the kids back and forth to school, instead of letting them ride the bus. Wherever she went, she paid careful attention to her surroundings. Hunter told her to inform the deputies of any excursions, no excuses. "Even if you want to walk around the property, let someone know," he stressed.

Hunter also reassured Shannon by making a daily phone call to check on her, setting a reminder on his iPhone. He tried to keep those conversations limited to a professional basis, asking if everything was all right or if anything new had occurred, but Shannon always managed to turn it around, somehow getting personal. She'd ask if he would come over to fix something after work or invite him to dinner to "thank him for looking after her and the children."

Hunter kept pondering this relationship. He was brought up to look after women and children in need of help, but he also knew how capable Shannon was. The best way to describe the impression he got was that Shannon needed too much help. To avoid being rude, he found a way to cut those calls short. "Got a beep and I need to take this call," he'd tell her so he could get off the phone.

On Saturday, his day off, Daryl took responsibility for watching Shannon and calling to check on her. This allowed Hunter to relax, and he fell asleep watching a basketball game on TV. When he awakened, he looked at the clock on the kitchen stove flashing six p.m. He yawned then stretched out his arms. He reached for his cell phone to check for any new messages, but the battery was dead.

After a brief search, he found the charging cord behind his chair. King liked to play with it and dragged it there. He plugged it in to charge as King ambled over to rub his trouser leg and meowed. Hunter sat up and peered at the cat's bright yellow eyes and asked, "You hungry, Boy? I'll fill your bowl." He went to the bedroom to check to see if he had any voicemails, but he found his house phone knocked off its base onto the floor in a couple of pieces.

"Damn you, King!" The cat at his bedroom door ran when the tone of his owner's voice made him realize he was in trouble.

Hunter sighed while putting the phone back together and placing it on its hook. "I really need to reach the office and check on Daryl." He stood. "Oh, well, at least I recorded the rest of that game." He filled King's food and water bowls, took out his car keys, and headed for the door. "I will be back in a minute," he said to King, "I'm going to use my car radio to reach the office. We can watch the rest of the game when I get back." He patted his stomach and then scratched the top of King's head.

"I'm hungry, too, King. I'll run down to the car, check on Daryl, and make this a quick trip."

That didn't happen.

When Hunter sat in his car and turned on the radio, he called Daryl. He then heard a frantic tone in Daryl's voice, "Hunter! I was about to drive to your place. Something is wrong at Shannon's. I called her at four p.m. but did not get a reply. I am headed that way now. See you there."

"Ten-four," said Hunter. He then raced up stairs to grab his cell phone and put on his badge. Rushing back down, he jumped into his police cruiser.

Dashing down Hwy 61 to the Tollar Plantation, Hunter and Daryl met up at the dirt road entrance to the property and parked in front of the house. "Been trying to phone you, Boss, but I couldn't get an answer. We got a frantic call from here, this time from Karla, but she was incoherent."

Hunter made a quick scan of the yard, "Well, it's clear nobody's home and Shannon's car is gone. I have told her repeatedly to let me know when she is leaving." It was frustrating, how could he protect her and the kids if they kept breaking protocol?

"Wait, Hunter, what is that?" Daryl pointed at something glaringly white in the dark interior of the cotton bin." Hunter then saw what Daryl was talking about. It was far enough away that he could not make it out.

"I don't know, let's check it out." Hunter followed his deputy, hand resting on his gun just in case.

As they walked into the dark interior of the building, Daryl gasped. "My God! Is that a child's body hanging there?" They ran toward it. Hunter tripped and stumbled forward, landing on his knees on the ground.

"I got it!" said Daryl as he ran past Hunter, eager to save the child, if that was what it was.

Shaking off the fall, Hunter got to his feet. "I'm okay," he said as he caught up to Daryl and saw what it was: not a body, but a large, white doll dangling above them, held up with rope.

Hunter brought over a ladder he spotted in the corner of the bin and Daryl climbed up on it and used his pocket knife to cut the rope. Now at eye level, they could see how it was mistaken for a body, but it wasn't. It was a large doll with the same coloring as Karla; dark hair, brown eyes stitched in, a nose, and light pink lips.

Hunter even thought the dress on the doll was one he had seen Karla wearing recently.

"Thank God!" Hunter exclaimed as the object fell to the floor. "I'm glad it wasn't Karla. This has to be Frederica's work. She's an insane psychopath trying to play tricks on us. Let's go. We've got to find her. The next time, it might be a real body." He took the doll with him and tossed it into his backseat.

Where to start the search was a problem. Hunter knew a mind like Frederica's worked differently from those of normal people. His experience with Rapier taught him that tough lesson, but how did hers work? Hunter took off his hat and ran his hand through his hair; he was hard-pressed to analyze that proposition. He sat in his patrol car and looked at the doll resting in the back seat. Who'd have thought to hang a doll in that bin? Where did she get one that large? An item like that was not available in Cleveland. Maybe this was where he needed to start.

First, though, he directed Daryl to put an all-points bulletin on Shannon's car. He had the license number written in the book he kept in his pocket, thank goodness. *But Frederica probably changed the plates. I'll give a description.* He relayed the information to Daryl who gave it to the operator.

Then Hunter told Daryl, "Call the First National Bank to see if Shannon's taken any money from the ATM in the last few hours. Then keep looking for that car. I am going to visit the shops in town to see if that doll could possibly have been bought in Cleveland. It's a wild shot, but we might get a lead from it. Those boutique stores in town carry all kinds of stuff."

At the Delta Collective, Hunter met with the shop owner who showed him a doll display in one of the rented booths, but it didn't have a doll that large. He visited two other stores: the Moonlight Flea Market and Maggie's Shop but got the same answer - nothing of the sort in their stock. Taking another look at the cryptic doll resting in the back of his patrol car, he decided to return to the plantation. Maybe they missed something.

It was dark when Hunter pulled up to the house for the second time that day and he noticed something was different. The living room light was on, shining brightly in the darkness. When he got out of his patrol car, he pulled out his flashlight and went to the front door. He was about to knock. Then he thought he heard a whimper from inside. He peeked through one of the antique glass windows on the side of the door and took in a breath.` He thought he saw Karla, hunched in the corner of the foyer, barely visible. He tried to turn the knob on the door but it was locked. He heard her whimper again and called to her through the front door, "Karla, it's me, Sheriff Harley. It's okay to let me in." *Is it? Could Frederica be lurking in another room?* He looked through the other windowpanes to see if anyone was near Karla.

Hunter then heard her weak voice. "I can't," Karla whimpered.

Hunter went back to the window where he first saw Karla and noticed when the child held up her hands, they were tied together with duct tape as were her ankles. A scarf was initially wrapped around her head to blindfold her, but she had managed to work it off and it hung around her neck.

Hunter went around to the back of the house and busted the window over the sink in the kitchen. He unlatched it and climbed into the house, pausing to hear if anyone else was inside. When no one appeared, he untied Karla, checking her for injuries, and asked, "Are you okay, Hon?"

Hunter helped her to stand, but her legs were shaky and she began to cry. When he tried to help her to the sofa, she balked. "Mama said not to move, to stay in the corner."

Hunter lifted her into his arms. "Look, I think she's gone. Karla, tell me exactly what happened. Where's Shannon and your brother? Do you know?" He sat beside her and put his arm around her shoulders.

She looked up at him, her eyes wet with tears. "I don't know. I'm hungry."

"I should have known. I'll get you something to eat and a drink. Then you can tell me everything. Wait right here."

In the kitchen, Hunter found a half-eaten pack of cinnamon rolls, took a Coke from the fridge, and brought them to Karla. He gave her a few minutes to gobble them down. "Now, what can you tell me?" he said.

Sucking in her bottom lip, Karla shook all over. "Mama came back. She grabbed Charles and held him like she did me the other day. He tried, but he couldn't get away. When Shannon pulled on him, Mama poked her in the eye."

"Where were you?"

"In the hall. I ran upstairs and called you from the house phone, but Mama said, 'Hang up or I'll kill Shannon and Charles.'"

"Did she have a gun?"

Karla bit her nails. "She said she did. I didn't see it."

"Okay, what happened next."

"Mama said she wanted more money. And Shannon said she didn't have any more. Mama got mad and socked her again. Shannon's mouth started bleeding and she couldn't get off the floor this time. Mama pulled her up and yelled to me. 'Come downstairs, Karla. I mean it!'"

Karla cried aloud. "I didn't know what to do. So I did what she said. Then she grabbed me, too. She stood over Shannon and told her, 'Get up; we're leaving here. You're going to find me some money somehow.' She said something about a machine at the bank." She shrugged. "I don't know what it was."

The child's tears were flowing and she was still shaking. Hunter gave her a moment as he tried to console her with fake promises. "Everything's going to be alright, Karla. Take a deep breath and then try to remember where you went. I'll find your mama, Shannon, and your brother. We'll make sure this will not happen   again."

What seemed like hours passed before Karla continued, but Hunter didn't rush her. Then she looked into Hunter's eyes and said, "We got in the car and went to the bank. Shannon got some money out of the machine out front and gave it to Mama. Then we drove around and around."

"Who was driving?

"Mama. We came back here and Mama put me in the corner and left with Charles and Shannon. Where'd she take them?" she sobbed out.

"I don't know yet, but I'll find out. How long ago do you think that was?"

"Not very long."

Hunter wracked his brain. *At least we know they're in Shannon's car and Karla didn't say anything about her mama changing the license plate. Maybe Daryl got something on the ATM withdrawal. I'll check with him. First, I have to get Karla to a safe place. I'll take her to Zita at the office.*

*   *   *

Hunter called Zita while he was on his way to the office with Karla. When he finally got there, Zita was there to greet the frightened child as Hunter watched her run into Zita's outstretched arms.

"Miss Zita, it was so horrible!"

"I know, dear, it's going to be okay. We will find everyone and make this right. You must be hot, let me take off your jacket."

When Zita helped Karla out of her jacket, she hung it up on the coat stand by the front door and a slip of paper fall out of the pocket

"Hunter, what is this?" Wide-eyed, she picked it up and unfolded it. Then she looked at Hunter and shook her head.

Chapter 7

Zita read the note that fell out of Karla's pocket aloud: *You'd better follow my orders or you'll never see Shannon and Charles again. I want more money. $10,000 more. I bet Shannon has some hidden; she was a rich lawyer in D. C. Find it. I mean it! You don't know who you're dealing with. I'll call and tell you where to leave it.*

She then handed the unsigned note to Hunter. It didn't have to be; he knew who wrote it. *But she's wrong on one count. I DO know who I'm dealing with. We all do.* Hunter's face turned red. *Just you wait, you…*No words could describe this woman who hurt and endangered her own children. *I'll get her and she's the one who's going to be sorry.*

When Hunter questioned Karla about the note, she hung her head. "I forgot about that. Mama's gonna be so mad with me." She rubbed her arms which both had dark bruises now.

Zita spoke up. "I won't let your mama hurt you again. Don't worry, Karla." She gave the little girl a hug and turned to Hunter.

"I've called DHR. They'll be here shortly. The social worker, Mrs. Istrada, goes to my church. I think I can convince her to let Karla stay with me for now."

"That would be a good solution."

Then Hunter got a call from Daryl. He didn't like the report he got. "Found Shannon's car on the side of the road at the Crossroads near her house. Nobody's in it. Dented on the passenger's side door. I've searched the area but no sign of anyone around."

"I'll send a tow truck." *Damn! Where the hell has that woman taken Shannon and Charles? If she's harmed them…No, I won't go there.* "Go to every house nearby and check to see if they saw anything, or know anything," he told Daryl. "I'll check out the car when it gets here."

Hunter met the truck at the holding lot and searched every inch of it. He checked under the seats, between the seats, and in the console and the glove compartment. Nothing, not even a paper wrapper. In a compartment next to the visor was a pair of prescription sunglasses. He also had the workers pop open the trunk and was relieved not to find a body in it. All he discovered was a briefcase full of Shannon's papers.

Hunter plopped down in the driver's seat. *How in the hell had Frederica managed to escape with an injured woman and a young boy in tow? Where had she gone? Was she holding someone else hostage in a house somewhere?* He scratched his ear. *Could she have stolen another car and left Cleveland? Would she leave without the money?*

A stroke of luck came when Zita called. Whiskers, the owner of the gas station just outside town near the Crossroads, reported a stolen car. He told her a tourist had left the motor running while he went to the restroom. When he returned to pump gas, the car was gone.

"Hunter, Whiskers thinks it will not be too hard to find the thief, One, the gas tank was empty; two, a pit bull was asleep on the floor in the back seat. The owner said the dog was old and deaf and may not have awakened if someone got into the back."

"Good to know," said Hunter, "At any rate, either Frederica–whom I feel sure was the thief–will either notice the gauge was on empty or run out of gas. Also, the dog is likely to awaken and start a ruckus, maybe jump free at the first opportunity. It gives me a glimmer of hope."

Hunter put out a Be On the Lookout for the license number the car owner gave them. Hunter headed to a highway out of town by the backroads. If anyone wanted to elude the police, that was the best choice. *She'll be in a pickle if she runs out of gas in a field away from nowhere.* He frowned. *But so will Shannon and Charles, and the old dog. She's not above putting them out of the car in an isolated area.* He slammed the steering wheel with his fist. *I've got to catch up to them, and fast. What else can go wrong?*

He soon thought of the answer to his question. It occurred to him that Frederica may have switched license plates and put Shannon's on the car she'd stolen. Then the plate and the car's description wouldn't match. If they were stopped by the police, they may just let them go. Hunter quickly called in the information, hoping he'd thought of it soon enough to prevent a fiasco. If not, he'd have himself to blame.

He drove down one street and up the other. Then he went to the Crossroads hoping to spot the missing person's car. Nothing, and nobody in sight even in the couple of barns he checked. *I've got to think like that woman. What would she do? If she sees her gas tank is empty, she'll stop at the next station. Maybe, just maybe, she'd go back to check on Karla. Not for Karla's sake, but to be sure we got her and the note. Hell, she'd have the nerve to stay at the Tollar Plantation thinking she could outwit us. I'll go there first.*

Hunter sped back to Shannon's. He pulled close to the house and hopped out of his patrol car. No car was parked nearby. He went to the porch and tried the door. It was still locked as they'd left it. So, he climbed through the broken window, calling out "Police." The first thing he saw was the photo of the kids with Santa Clause back in its place. By the bottom of the frame was another note, it read: *Ha, I outwitted you again, Sheriff. Look for the money while you're here. I'm giving you another day. Then you better have it and follow my orders.* He held it by the corner and put it in a plastic bag, then into his pocket. He didn't search for any money, but he did search the house and the cotton bin, still finding no clues except food was missing. No empty milk cartons or other containers. She'd taken those with her so as not to leave evidence.

But why would she care about fingerprints? They already knew who she was.

Hunter had to rethink the situation. Frederica didn't think like most people. *That's good in a way. It may make her more vulnerable.* Still, he had no illusions about outwitting her. She walked her own path, and nobody could second guess where it would lead. Hunter felt the need of a psychiatrist's input, but he didn't trust their judgment either. He had to rely on his own gut instincts. They usually served him best.

Leaving the house, Hunter blamed himself for missing an opportunity. Why hadn't he left an officer there on duty. He knew it was because no sane person would return to that house. But Frederica didn't fit in the "sane" category.

Hunter left the Tollar Plantation, just realizing the sun was close to setting. He didn't realize how late it was or how exhausted he felt. He had to get a couple of hours rest. First, though, he had to catch up with Frederica. Nature didn't let him complete that task. Ten minutes later, his eyes fell shut and he drove towards a tall pine tree on the side of the road.

Hunter didn't know how long he'd been unconscious until he looked at his watch—only half an hour. He opened the car's door and was able to stand on his feet. In the outside mirror, he saw blood trickling down from his forehead, but he felt the area and it was only a cut. He realized he must have hit his head on the steering wheel. He wiped off the blood with a tissue he pulled from his pocket and walked to the front to check the damage. It wasn't bad. Mostly his front bumper dented in. Some bark was scraped off of the tree when it slowed his car down. He was glad he wasn't going very fast. No matter, he had to report the accident. And his crew didn't need this added to their concerns. He called it in, minimizing it as much as possible.

"You should've gone home to get some rest sooner, Hunter," Zita chided him. "You're not a robot, you know. Now, go get yourself checked out."

"No, I'm fine. I will go get some rest, but first I need to know if there's any news about Frederica, before I call the FBI and get them involved."

"Sorry. Nobody has seen that stolen car. Look, put this aside till you can think straight. We can take care of things."

Feeling a little weak-kneed, Hunter went to his house. He first went to the bathroom to clean up the dried blood on his forehead, expecting a bruise there in the morning. Before sleeping, though, he fed King, and he had a ham sandwich and a glass of milk. "Old boy," he told the cat, "if I could get you on this case, I bet you'd solve it in a few minutes."

The cat meowed and resumed eating. Hunter climbed into bed on top of his covers, put his phone on silent, and was asleep in a few minutes. He remained there until King jumped right in his face. He looked at his clock and realized he had slept till 10 am. He was in no rush, taking his time getting ready.

When he looked at his phone, he realized he missed calls, but they'd left messages. It was a voicemail from Zita: "Hunter, get down here right away. We have some new developments. V's here and he says he has information about Frederica, but he won't tell us anything."

Chapter 8

At the station, V sat in a chair by the front door wearing his usual "uniform" of shorts and a T top. He rose to shake Hunter's hand when he came in the door. "Got some news for you, Sheriff. Didn't know you were home, or I'd have come upstairs." He chuckled. "Zita tried to drag it out of me, but I held back. I wouldn't tell anybody but you. I don't think anyone else would believe me, but you might."

"No problem, let's go into my office where we can have privacy." said Hunter, noticing the look of frustration on Zita's and Daryl's faces as they passed by.

Suspense consumed Hunter as they walked into his office and closed the door behind them, but he knew it was crucial to be patient with this eccentric. *He's far from being like Frederica but he has his own ways. He takes his time and he won't be pushed. When he has something to say, he'll say it.* Hunter nodded.

Making two fists, V blurted out, "Someone chopped an ear off of the cat."

"What?" Pictures of King bleeding where an ear was missing flashed through his mind. Stepping close to V, Hunter said in a loud voice, "King was fine when I left a few minutes ago. How could…"

"No, not King." V backed away. "I mean my cat sculpture. You know, the one I made from metal parts? It stands about three feet tall. They knocked off the ear. They put a piece of paper in its hollow body. I slipped it out from the bottom."

Hunter sighed. "Okay, how's this connected to Frederica?"

V pulled the piece of paper out of his pocket and handed it to Hunter. He read the note. *Put the cat out front tomorrow so Hunter can leave the money in the other ear. I'll take $5000 and give you a week to get the other half. It better be there by 6 p.m. or somebody's going to pay.*

Hunter slipped the note in an evidence bag and asked V for details about what happened and when. He didn't have any. V didn't know how or when Frederica got inside his shop to do the damage to the sculpture and leave the note. He never saw her. That wasn't unusual because V had a habit of sculpting in the back until a customer rang his bell. Then he'd go wait on them in the front room. The cat sculpture was kept in the front area.

It struck Hunter that Frederica wasn't scared off. She wouldn't leave town until she got some money, maybe all $10,000. If they paid off the $5,000, what would happen next? Would she release Shannon and Charles, or would it lead to their murder?

"V," Hunter said, "please put the cat sculpture outside like the note says. We've got to figure this out and see the best course of action. I don't know if we can get $5,000 by tomorrow, but we'll let you know."

V pulled out a wad of cash. "Here's $3,000. Can you get the rest? I don't want to see anything happen to those kids, or Shannon."

He tried to press the money into Hunter's palm, but Hunter shook his head and handed it back. "Thanks. I can't take that, but it's very generous of you. Look, I'll get back with you if it comes to a crunch. You'll really be helping by putting, er, King, Jr., outside." Opening his office door, Hunter entered the lobby. "Time for me to get to work. You go on back home, V; I know where to find you and I'll keep you posted."

V caught Hunter's arm and met him eye to eye, "There's one more thing you ought to know. I didn't think it was important at the time, but now who knows? I had this old guitar for sale in my shop. I was planning on painting it, but Shannon was interested in it. She picked it up and started playing right away, by ear. I had to sell it to her after that; it looks like she inherited Goldie's talent. When she sang Goldie's *I'm Only Human* for me, it was easy to see that she's a natural."

"Now that's a surprise! She didn't say anything and I didn't see it at her house. I guess it's in her genes."

V stroked his beard. "You know, she is clever; I thought she might find a way through music to leave you a clue." He opened both palms. "I know that's a stretch, but I wanted to tell you, just in case. Look, I even got her to let me record it on my phone. I left it back at my shop. You want to hear it? "

"I sure do."

V laughed. "I hope you'll react better than Charles did. He was there when she sang it and he said, 'That's crazy. Everybody's human.' Okay, I'll meet you there in ten minutes."

At V's shop, surrounded by various sculptures and paintings in process, he brought up the file and played the music for Hunter. Shannon's talent shined through when she sang the last song , the one Goldie had written long ago. The final verse came through with a powerful passion:

Life will soon end

This world is not my friend

I miss my woman.

Won't be here long

And so I sing this song

I'm only human,

I'm only human.

Hunter could tell by the lyrics Goldie knew he was going to die soon. Even a tough guy like him reacted to the vibes that came down through the ages. *Creepy.* He didn't say anything; he just turned his head and swallowed hard.

"Well," V asked, "what do you think?"

"She's damn good."

"She could be a star." V shook his head. "But I'm not sure she wants that. She's wrapped up in taking care of those kids, and she's got her law practice, such as it is."

She can't be anything if we don't find her. Hunter didn't express that thought to V; he had to move on. "First we have to rescue her and Charles," he said. "You need help getting that cat sculpture out front?"

"Yeah. It's not heavy, but it's a little awkward."

Hunter took one side and V had the other. They manipulated the work of art to a position by the front door. Then V secured it to a hook on the wall he'd put there for such purposes. He had a price of $1,895.00 on it, but he didn't plan to sell it. That was just to avoid paying taxes on it as inventory.

Hunter looked at the cat's ear. *Frederica has sized this up. She knows it's big enough to hold a large envelope and that it can be stuffed down in the canal and nobody will likely spot it. She's nutty, but tricky, and shrewd.*

His cell phone rang. "We've got a lead, Boss," Daryl said. "A guy at the Get-'n-Go store on the way to the Crossroads phoned and he says he may have seen that stolen car."

Hunter told V what was going on and rushed to his patrol car. "How long ago? I'm on my way."

"About ten minutes."

"Ten-four." As Hunter traveled the familiar road, , he speculated on what this might lead to–maybe finding Shannon and Charles; maybe nothing. Using his siren, he sped to the scene and parked in the lot in record time.

As Hunter got out of his car to go inside the Get 'n Go store, he noticed a scraggly dressed man standing on the side of the building, just beyond the public pay phone.

"Sheriff," a man waved and called out. He took a step back, "Come over here."

Hunter complied, but he was confused. He'd thought the clerk at the convenience store had called in. Instead, it seemed that it was this stranger. Hunter didn't recognize the man, so he moved closer, hand resting on his gun. He followed as the man backed up to where others could not see them. He noticed the bottle in his hand and no doubt the stranger had whiskey on his breath. It was obvious this man was homeless and an alcoholic.

"Hey man, you got my attention. Were you the one who called the police with a tip?"

The man nodded, "My name's Dewayne Roi. I'm on my way back to Jackson. Been bummin' around, doing odd jobs. It's hard traveling through the Delta, not enough work. I came here to get some cigarettes, but I saw somethin' strange." He reached into his pocket and pulled out a plastic ID card and handed it to Hunter before he could ask for identification.

Strange, thought Hunter as he looked closely at the ID card. The address was a post office box in Kosciusko, Mississippi. His age was fifty-two, but he looked much older.

Dwayne paused to take a puff on his cigarette as Hunter looked around. "I guess you're just here to get cigarettes, right? I don't see your car. From the looks of that bottle in your hand, you don't need to be driving anyway."

"No worries, Sheriff, I don't have no car. I walked here." He nodded toward a field. "I been stayin' in that old barn over there to rest up a couple o' days. I plan to move on, maybe tomorrow. Anyways, I just paid for my cigarettes when I saw this car pull up through the glass. Two women and a boy get out. The driver then grabs onto the boy's arm and the other woman–she looked afraid–she stays on the kid's other side. The driver, hey, she looked rough, no better'n me. The other lady, she had on nicer clothes. It was weird. So, I buy a cup o' coffee and hang around a few minutes. I slipped toward the back of the store so they didn't notice me."

"First, the driver comes in, bringing everyone with her, and pays cash to fill her tank. The boy says 'I'm hungry; I want some chips' and he picks up a candy bar. She yells, "No, and if you're really hungry, you can wait and get real food, not junk.'" Dwayne scratched his unruly beard. "That kid looked bright, but he said somethin' kinda' odd: 'I'm only human, Mama. I'm a kid and we like candy." She pulled him to her and slapped his face, but he didn't shut up. The nice dressed lady stepped forward, but then backed off when the other lady looked at her.

The boy repeated *I'm only human*, looking at me and then at the clerk. Then she hustles everyone into the family restroom, you know the big one where moms can change their babies diapers, and I seen her shake her fist at the other lady as she dragged her in."

Dewayne nodded. "I've got a radio, a Deputy Zita described two missing people and how to call if anyone sees anything. I thought it might be them." He narrowed his eyes. "I got the feelin' that woman driving knew the clerk. I think she handed him a note when he gave her a receipt." He pulled out a crumpled envelope. "So, I walked outside and wrote down their license number while they were in the restroom, and I called the station after they drove off using the pay phone." He handed the license number to Hunter.

Hunter took a deep breath. *Yes! It's Shannon's license plate. Frederica must have put it on the stolen car. But what did Charles mean by saying he's only human?* Then those words hit him. It was the title of the song they found of Goldie's. He didn't reveal all of his discoveries. Instead, he said, "Those are the two we're looking for. You need to stay here in Cleveland a couple more days in case I need to talk to you. Can you promise me you'll do that?"

"Be glad to. Barn owner won't know. Found out he's out of town visiting relatives. Say," he narrowed his eyes, "could you loan me a couple o' bucks? Maybe ten? I'll need money if I stay here without a job."

Hunter handed him the only cash he had–a twenty dollar bill. It might assure he'd hang around. "I'm checking with the cashier, but I'll get back with you. I know where to find you. You can go now."

Dewayne crossed the dirt road and returned to the field of the barn he'd made home. Hunter paid attention to where he went so he could find the man later.

Going inside, Hunter tipped his hat to the clerk who introduced himself as Judas Martin, also new in town, but he'd been working at this store almost a month, he said. Thinking the name Martin also sounded familiar, Hunter asked, "You related to any Martins around here? Seems like I've heard that name before."

The man shrugged. "Don't think so. Say, I saw you talkin' to Dewayne. He comes over here to charge his police scanner. What's going on?"

Ha, so he saw me talking to Dewayne, did he? Hunter debated how much to tell him and decided to reveal as little as possible. "He called in a report about a couple of women and a boy who were here acting a little odd. You know those folks?"

"Nope." He poked out his bottom lip. "Never saw them before."

"He said the woman slapped the boy's face. Did you   see   that?"

"Naw, I wasn't looking." He shifted from foot to foot.

Lie number one. Never having seen the woman before might also be a lie. Judas—what a moniker to put on a kid. But it sounds like the name fits the character. It's appropriate. He's sure acting suspicious.

Hunter leaned across the counter and glared at Judas. "Didn't that woman hand you a note?"

Red-faced, Judas glared back at him. "Back off! Why the hell would a woman I don't know give me a note? I'm done!" He slammed his fist on the countertop. "Now, Sheriff, either arrest me or get out of here."

Since Hunter didn't have enough on the man to make an arrest, he turned to leave, but not before saying, "I'll be back. You can count on it." *Something is amiss here. Nobody reacts that way unless they have something to hide. Yeah! I'll mull on this for a while. Maybe the name connection will come to me. Then I can come back with a warrant.*

Not knowing what else he could do to help find Shannon and Charles and not wanting to go back home to the office, he decided to drive down the dirt road in the direction of the Crossroads remembering how a famous singer sold his soul for success in music and how that same man tried to get Goldie to follow his lead. But Goldie resisted. Because of his love for Eleanor, he didn't succumb to the temptation of wealth and fame and the price he'd have to pay for it. He also didn't live long enough to do that. *Martin* wove its way to invade Hunter's thoughts. He couldn't find a first name to fit, nor could he think of any other connection–until his mind backed up over half a century to focus on cold case files, specifically Goldie Parsons.

Chapter 9

In life, there are those things that eat at the side of a person's mind, cluing that person into something not quite realized. Hunter was having one of those moments. Why did the name of the new clerk bother him so much? Then: Boom!

Hunter grasped his steering wheel with both hands, trying to keep his car on the road as a revelation hit him. *Wylie Martin. That's the blues singer who tried to tempt Goldie into selling his soul to the devil. Could Judas be a relative, a grandson or great grandson? Man, now that would be a connection. The name was common enough, but a connection was possible..*

Rain poured down along with a heavy fog. Hunter's windshield wipers were going full speed, but he still could barely see the dirt road in front of him. He slowed down and edged forward since the road was slowly turning into mud. In a flash of lightning crossing the sky, a drenched figure appeared on his right a football field length ahead of him. *Could that be Shannon? Or is it wishful thinking and am I seeing things?*

He didn't have time to analyze his thoughts. A loud pop caused him to stop the car. In the heavy rain, Hunter got out to see what was wrong. He pulled his Stetson hat down tight on his head and put on his raincoat as he got out of the car to see what was wrong, but he already had an idea of the cause. The right front tire was flat. Aiming his flashlight at it, he saw the fender had been dented when he ran into the tree and it must have damaged the tire. With a sigh, he returned to the driver's seat, called in the problem, and asked for help in case the figure he saw was real. Maybe it was Shannon.

Hunter took out the spare tire and made the replacement. A patrol car with Zita driving passed by following up on the figure. All the while, his thoughts turned to what was going on. *If that was Shannon, I've probably missed my chance to catch up with her. Where's Charles and Frederica? Good God, I hope Zita makes it there fast. Maybe there's still a chance…*

Before Hunter could leave the scene, Zita pulled up beside him in her patrol car. "Hey, Boss, you okay? Got the tire fixed?"

Hunter nodded. "I'm fine. Did you find the person I thought I saw?"

Zita shook her head. "I drove quite a ways, but I didn't see Shannon, or anyone else But whoever it is needs help. It's not safe on this road, especially in this kind of weather.

Hunter said, "Let's try again. I'll follow you."

Zita sped away and Hunter got into his driver's seat, ready to roll. When he pulled forward, his back tire spun and the car didn't move. "Damn it to hell!" he screamed to the wind. He got out again and surveyed the scene. Both back tires had sunk into the muck when he'd pulled off on the soggy side of the road. He felt foolish not to have checked earlier. He radioed Zita and told her to continue the hunt, that he'd been delayed. He didn't explain why.

Hunter then remembered what he had in the trunk to help this situation, cat litter! He'd recently read that cat litter can help get a car out of the mud by providing traction in this sort of situation. As the rain started to slack off, he popped the trunk. But he tussled with the bag and it slit open as he pulled it out. Cat litter fell all over, not just in the area where it was needed.

Stumbling around, he stepped into a deep groove of tire tracks, causing water to splash all over his boots and the bottom of the uniform pants he'd picked up from the dry cleaners the day before. Hunter wondered how many bad things could happen to him in a day. It reminded him of the idiom, "If I didn't have bad luck, I'd have none at all." *What the devil can come next?*

He soon found out. When he followed the tracks to the barn, the door was wide open. He could see that a car had driven in there and backed out in a hurry. Another set of tracks led away from the building. Keeping his hand on his holster, he checked around and called out, "Dewayne, are you in here?"

Then Hunter's foot hit something–a human body. With that stimulation came a groan. Hunter helped Dewayne stand up as he was rubbing his bleeding forehead. "She smacked me with a shovel," he blurted out. "Knocked me out cold." He stood, swaying back and forth. Hunter grabbed his arm to keep him upright.

Hunter flashed the light upward to inspect his wound. The blood had dried, so the attack must have been a while ago. "Who hit you with a shovel?"

"That woman you're lookin' for. The one drivin' the car and she came in the store." He lowered his head to his chin. "Oh, God. I ain't neva had a headache this bad with a hangover." He looked up. "You got a aspirin, or somethin' stronger, Sheriff? My head's killin' me."

"I'll take you to the hospital, but first tell me what happened. Do you know where there went? "

Dewayne pressed his temples. "Lemme think. She woke me up when she drove into the barn, I slipped behind a bale of hay in the corner when I realized who it was. She told them other two to stay in the car and she gets out and starts pokin' around." He pointed to the blade of a machete laying in the dirt. "She picked that up but threw it down when she saw it didn't have no handle. Then she spotted me and we got into a tussle—man was she strong!" He pointed to a corner. "Then she grabbed that shovel and swung it at me."

He shrugged. "Don't know how, but it didn't get me right away. The other woman hopped out of the car with the kid right behind her and they headed for the door. The boy tripped and the woman left me, grabbed his leg and pulled him back, tossing him in the back seat of the car. Whoo-eeh! She backed outta here so fast the other lady didn't have a chance to do nothin'. She tried to chase the car. 'Course she had no way to stop it, but she ran off and didn't come back. I guess I musta passed out then; I don't remember no more."

He swayed again and Hunter helped him to the corner to sit on the bale of hay. This injured drunk couldn't possibly help him with his car. Male pride be damned. Outside help was his only recourse. He got on his cell phone, ordered an ambulance, and reported everything, including his car being stuck. He also asked what Zita found out. The "Nothing yet. 10-4," reply was devastating. He'd hoped Shannon was the figure on the highway and that she'd been rescued, even if Charles was still in danger in the grip of Frederica.

But nothing else had worked out today; why should he expect anything to do so now? It was one time when Hunter wished he had the faith of his deputy Zita. At least then he could pray that Shannon hadn't been recaptured by Frederica. But he had to admit that was the most likely possibility. Just in case help was in a deity, Hunter recalled what Zita, a Catholic, did in such emergencies. Mimicking her actions, he made the Sign of the Cross. While mouthing the words, *In the name of the Father, the Son, and the Holy Ghost,* it struck him that those same words were associated with the Mojo. *Ha, if one doesn't work, maybe the other will. Mojo, do your stuff. Amen.*

The arrival of the ambulance, fire truck, and police in sequence interrupted Hunter's thoughts. They put Dewayne into the ambulance and one officer finishing taping off the area said, "They got your car out of the rut, Sheriff. You're set to go. It's still raining. Get in and I'll drive you back to the highway."

Hunter took charge. "You finish up here. I'll walk back to my car."

He poked his head in the ambulance's back door. "I'll check on you later, Dewayne. We've still got some talking to do."

Now on an IV, Dewayne replied. "Shore. I'll get a good night's sleep in a bed for a change. Ain't had one in a while. You know where to find me."

Cracking a smile, Hunter left. Back at his car, he thanked the men who'd pulled his car free and headed down the highway. Checking on his radio, he still got a negative report from Zita. No sight of Shannon or her car. Maybe that figure was just a figure of his imagination. No matter. Whether she was on the road or still Frederica's prisoner, he had to find her. He braked at the Crossroads and stared as far as he could in all directions–nothing moving in sight, not even a deer or a raccoon. Silence was deafening. The only sound was his ringing ears.

Hunter widened his eyes as a place to look popped into his head like a vision. If he could find that structure, he might find Shannon. It was a long shot, but one he had to take.

Chapter 10

He'd only seen that small house once. But it was unusual, so it stuck in his mind. It had enough space to provide shelter. He felt it was significant and was determined to find it. Why it was in the middle of a field with no other house nearby and who put it there had tweaked his curiosity. At the time, it wasn't important. Now, it might be. He racked his brain, trying to recreate the scene he'd passed by once while driving fifty miles per hour. He turned right and drove fifteen miles per hour, staring in first one direction and then another at every field he passed, slowing or pausing to peek behind any stands of trees.

It occurred to him if Shannon came across the house, she may not have been able to get to it. Then again, he realized she was very resourceful, so she'd try. It would be a good hiding place. He hoped it wasn't so good that he couldn't find it.

Coming upon a spot that seemed familiar, he pulled over but not far enough to get stuck again. Then he got out of the car and headed behind some bushes.

The rain had slowed to a drizzle but he still had on his raincoat. Farther from the road than he'd recalled, he saw a huge oak tree and headed for it taking large steps. When he reached the base of the tree, he looked upward.

Aha! I found it! Now I have to see if anyone's in it. "Anybody there?" He called out. "This is the Sheriff. Come down if you're up there. That's an order!"

He stepped on the bottom rung of the make-shift ladder, ready to ascend, but he didn't have to. In five seconds, Shannon descended the rickety tree house as fast as she could. "Hunter, am I glad to see you! I've been up there for hours wondering if Frederica would discover where I was. "

On the bottom step, she fell into Hunter's arms sobbing. "It's been so horrible." She backed away. "Have you found Charles, and Frederica? Please say you have!"

Hunter wished he could but he had to shake his head. "We're still looking. Don't worry; we'll find them. Karla's fine. A deputy is with her." He visually checked Shannon for injuries. She had none visible, but her pants were torn and she had dirt all over her body. "Are you okay?" he asked.

"Physically, yes. Mentally, no. Oh, did you find Karla?'

"Yes, she's fine. Zita's taking care of her. Look, I'm calling for an ambulance…"

"No! I don't need one. All I need is a shower and a change of clothes. Take me home. I'll tell you everything that happened on the way. Then we can look for Charles. I have an idea where Frederica may take him. She still has that stolen car."

They got to the patrol car and drove toward the Tollar plantation while Shannon related all that happened. Her story matched Dewayne's. She added that Frederica tried to run her down while driving off with Charles. "She missed me by inches when I dropped to the ground and rolled out of target range." Her hand shook as she told about the incident.

"I knew I couldn't catch a moving car, but it was my chance to escape, so I took it and kept running. I stayed off of the highway most of the time and wandered through the fields. I thought I'd be harder to find there." Her bottom lip quivered. "Once, I went back to get my bearings, but I saw a car and darted back into the woods."

"That was me," Hunter interjected. "I was looking for you until I got stuck in the mud. Zita took over but couldn't find you."

She patted Hunter's knee. "I'm glad *you* found me."

Hunter brushed her hand aside. *Not now, Shannon. Don't start anything.* He looked out of the window checking fields for her car until they reached her house. He followed her inside and checked everything out. Nothing was disturbed. The corner where Karla had been tied up reminded him of what that child had gone through, but he didn't tell Shannon those disturbing details. It could wait until later. Instead, he pulled out his cell phone and contacted the FBI. They said they'd send two agents right away. Then he checked in at the office, gave his report, and ended the conversation with "Over and out," just as Shannon came into the living room in Jeans and a blue slipover top. Her shiny red hair combed with every strand in place. She sparkled.

"Wow! It feels so good to be clean again." She went to the kitchen and grabbed a bag of chips and two Cokes. "I'm hungry." She handed him a Coke and held out the chips. "Have some."

He took the offering. "I guess I'm hungry, too. It's been a long night. Look, Shannon, I've ordered a deputy to guard your house. I don't think I can function any longer. As soon as I talk to the FBI agents, I'm going home to get some sleep. Why don't you do the same?"

She wrinkled her nose. "But I got all dressed to go with you. I can't sleep. I need to see Karla and find Charles."

Hunter shook his head. "Karla's fine with Zita. She's probably already asleep. We both need rest. I'm leaving. You go to bed." He walked out of the door, got into his car, and drove off. Shannon stood in her doorway staring at his car pulling away, but she didn't wave goodbye.

Back at the station, he met two FBI members. "Marian Moore." The female agent held out her hand and shook Hunter's.

"I'm Agent Jean Guidry. My name is pronounced John, but it's spelled J-e-a-n. Got that?" He lifted his chin and his demeanor reminded Hunter of Carlton, especially when he added, "We'll take over from here."

Hunter sucked in his breath. *I can't handle another one of those. You may think you'll take over, but I'm staying on the case.* After bringing the two agents looking like high school students up to date on the case, Hunter left. He didn't expect much help from them, but the upside was, because of lack of experience, they probably wouldn't interfere too much.

The minute Hunter opened his door, King came trotting up and meowing. "Hi, Boy," Hunter greeted him. "I'll get you food and water." He came back with filled bowls and King ignored both. He meowed and followed Hunter to the bedroom where he undressed as the cat circled his legs and rubbed against them.

"Oh, I guess you've been lonely. He reached down and petted the cat who swatted at his hand and scratched it. "Whoa! You can't do that even if you're mad with me." He picked up a magazine and gave King a light lick. "Now don't try that again," he said as King scurried back to his bowls and gobbled down food and water. Knowing cat scratches are more dangerous than a dog bite, Hunter washed the wound and dabbed Neosporin on it.

After taking a shower, dressed in his pajamas, Hunter fixed himself a bologna sandwich which he washed down with a glass of milk. He got into bed and

King came back and snuggled beside him, waiting to get his tummy scratched. Hunter complied. "I knew you wouldn't stay mad long. You're a good boy."

His thoughts turned to Charles. Was he safe? He took some consolation in knowing Charles was very smart. But he was still a young boy who'd be hard-pressed to outwit a schemer like Frederica. Hunter yawned. *I can't fix that tonight. At least Shannon and Karla are safe. Tomorrow I'll find Charles.* King meowed as if in agreement. Hunter scratched his tummy again and in minutes they both fell asleep.

*   *   *

At six a.m., the alarm clock awakened Hunter and King. The cat jumped off of the bed, and Hunter sat up with a jolt. *Is it morning already? Seems like I just went to sleep.* He swung his legs across the side of the bed and checked his cell phone. No messages. No emergencies, but no good news either. He ambled to the kitchen and fried bacon and eggs while the coffee perked. Gulping down a small glass of orange juice, he popped a piece of rye bread into the toaster. It didn't toast. Checking it, he chuckled as he plugged it in. Putting the vittles on a Dixie paper plate, he sat down to take his first bite. Then his phone rang, so he went to the bedroom to retrieve it.

"Hunter, Shannon called," Zita said. "She wants me to bring Karla to her. I thought I should clear that with you. Will Karla be safe at home?"

"She's up early, isn't she? I have a deputy posted at Shannon's house, but don't do anything until I get there. Look, let me set things straight. We have to cater to those FBI agents, but tell them as little as possible and don't cut them any more slack than necessary."

"Ten-four about that. They left thirty minutes ago. That'll keep them busy for a while. Back to Shannon, she said if I couldn't bring Karla home, she'd order a rental car and she'd come to get her. What then?"

"She won't get a rental instantly. She is forgetting she is in Cleveland, Mississippi. I'll call John, he runs the office, and have him delay it till after I get to the office. He owes me a favor."

"Ten-four. I'll get Karla up and give her breakfast, then we'll come to the office. Give me about forty-five minutes."

Hunter went back to his breakfast and ate the lukewarm food. He was hungry enough to manage it not being steaming hot as he liked it. He refilled King's bowls, dressed in a fresh uniform, and a clean pair of boots. It felt good to be clean and dry. Weather reports said no rain predicted today. Maybe he could stay comfortable.

On the short walk to the office, he analyzed the situation and made a plan. First, he had to work around the FBI agents and deal with Shannon to decide what would be best for Karla. He came to the conclusion that she'd be safe with Shannon as long as a deputy stayed on duty at their house. Next, he mulled over where to look for Frederica and Charles. In her frame of mind, and with her erratic behavior, that was difficult to determine. It would all be guesswork, but he had to make the attempt.

Once again, he tried to put himself in her place and think like she thought. But their brains were wired differently and the chore seemed impossible. It stymied him because he had no past record to judge by. No clues at all as to her previous actions. Besides, this situation was different. Frederica may have been the kids' biological mother, but she was acting more like their worst enemy. She'd slapped Charles and thrown him in the car. Worse yet, she'd tied up her little daughter and left her without nourishment. Karla could have died. That showed Frederica was capable of murder.

Heads turned as Hunter flung open the station's door and it banged against the wall behind it. His stern expression became a frown which brought the room to silence. *The buck stops with me. I'm the one who has to resolve this. Look out, Frederica, you damn fool. Whatever it takes, I'm coming to get you. I'll find you, and I'll snatch that boy from your grasp. I'm going to bring Charles home safe and sound!*

Chapter 11

Zita followed Hunter into his office. "We've got a problem," she said. "Shannon called and said she got a phone call ordering her to have the money, $10,000, in the sculpture's ear by ten a.m. She doesn't have that much in the bank."

"That's okay. She'll take less than the full amount of ransom. My plan is to only have real money on the top. The rest can be newspapers. We can put security all over the place on the street and in V's shop. I'll talk to the FBI agents right away and let them think it's their idea. That'll appease them. We'll catch Frederica and free Charles."

"Frederica must have a partner. This time, Shannon said it sounded like a man's voice on the phone."

Hunter sat on the edge of his desk. "That might complicate matters, but we outnumber them. We'll request more help from the feds, too. All right. Let's get busy. Pick up Shannon and take her to the bank. Leave

Karla here at the station. They can both stay home afterwards."

"Shannon won't like that a bit."

"Doesn't matter. Tell her she has to stay out of this. After the money drop, take her home with Karla and insist that they don't budge from their house. They must not even go outside. Convince her this is the best way to save Charles, and them." He grinned. "At least she won't have a car to run off in. John took care of that. "

"She may call Jackson to get a car."

"That'll still delay things. Jackson is a good four hours away, until after the scheduled pick-up." He motioned to the door with his thumb. "Now, get going. We don't have much time."

When Zita reached the Tollar Plantation, Shannon stood at the front door. "Where's Karla?" she asked.

"At the station. We'll pick her up after we go to the bank."

"I don't like this," Shannon complained, but she went along. She didn't have any choice.

As they reached the car, Zita told Shannon the plan and added, "Just withdraw two hundred dollars in twenty-dollar bills. That's all we'll need to make it look like the rest is there."

"What? No! You want her to kill Charles? You're crazy. I'm giving her as much as I can." Tears flooded her cheeks which had turned red. "You know what can happen. That woman's psycho. She won't hesitate to get revenge if she's cheated."

Zita kept calm. "Get into the car, Shannon. We don't have time to argue. We need to get to the bank. It's already 9:15."

Shannon plopped down on the passenger's seat in front and snapped on her seat belt. "This is my little brother we're talking about. He's in danger. You can't tell me what to do."

Taking a deep breath, Zita spoke softly. "I have to. The FBI is in on this now. They plan to take charge, Shannon, and we will all need to use our best chance to stop Frederica and her accomplice, if she has one. It's Charles' best chance for survival, too." She pulled up at the bank without admitting Hunter's plan to stay on top of things. "You go inside alone and I'll wait right here."

Frowning, Shannon went in and moved from foot to foot as she waited for four people ahead of her to be served. Then she got her money, returned to the car, and handed the envelope to Zita. She didn't say a word until they reached the station and Karla ran up to her when she entered.

"Take me home, Shannon," she begged.

"I will, Honey, right now."

Zita whispered to Shannon, "I've stuffed the envelope. You have to walk down the street and put the money in the cat's ear yourself. I understand Frederica knows you've contacted the police, but it may set her off to see one of us doing that. Go on and come straight back here and we'll send you and Karla home.

Zita tried to see if anyone was watching but couldn't tell. It shocked her when Shannon took the paper out of the envelope, stuffed it in her large purse, and replaced it with real bills. While she walked to the sculpture, Zita noted everyone who passed--a woman with two kids in tow, a teenager, and as Shannon left and turned back, Zita spotted a man on a bike with a kid on its crossbar. Both wore hoods, so she couldn't see their faces. The man paused and the kid petted the cat's metal head. Then they moved on, turning the first corner.

V rushed out of his shop and yelled, "They got the money!" Deputies converged upon the scene from everywhere. The two FBI agents had returned and got in on the act. Hunter arrived in his car first. He didn't stop. He skidded around the first corner and that's when he discovered they'd dumped the bike. Except for an unoccupied parked car, he didn't see a vehicle in sight. He called in ordering his deputies to search in every direction on foot and in their patrol cars, and he headed for the highway. If Frederica had a partner who'd picked up her and Charles, he'd take them somewhere to hide, but where?

Shannon ran back to the station and banged on the first desk she came to. "This was bound to happen. I'm glad I switched the paper for money. Maybe the $5,000 will satisfy them. There's two of them; I know it." She looked all around. "Where's Hunter? Where's Zita? Oh, hell! There's something I haven't told them." She stared at Chan. "Find them. Get one of them on their radio. This may be our last chance."

Karla squeezed a stuffed bear they'd given her. Shannon picked her up and held her close. "It's okay. We're going to get Charles back. Don't you worry."

Zita came into the room and Shannon hurried toward her. "Look, I know something that may help." They went into Zita's office and Shannon sat down with Karla in her lap. She lit right into her revelation. "For about a month now, I've been getting calls from a man saying he's a rightful owner of the record we found of Goldie's. He wants me to sell it and give him the money, all of it. He even told me his name, Judas Martin. His claim is that his great-grandfather, Wylie Martin, was Goldie's partner in that endeavor and he coauthored the songs. He said he's going to sue me if he has to."

She took a deep breath. "I ignored him, but when he called with a threat to Charles and Karla this morning, I got worried. He even said he knew about another song and if I had it, I'd better give it to him. I realized they might be working together yesterday, so I got in my rental car and went to his store. I brought my pistol."

Hunter's head jerked back. "Whoa! Rental car?'

The corner of Shannon's lip curled. "Yep. I knew you'd try to block me from renting a car, so I used another name. I walked a block or two to meet the guy who delivered the car early this morning."

I didn't get to John in time. She outwitted me. Oh, what the hell!

"*Anyhow, Judas* lied and denied any connection, but he stood his ground and said he was going to get his money, one way or another. He ordered me to leave and when I wouldn't, he came around the counter and tried to manhandle me."

A smile curled the corners of Shannon's lips. "I lived in a few rough places before I came to Cleveland. I learned a few tricks; a girl has to protect herself. When he reached for me, I grabbed his arm, jerked it behind his back and twisted it, threatening to break it if he made a false move. He broke free and I shoved him against the wall, pulled out my gun, and stuck it in his face. It was my turn to make a threat. I screamed at him, 'Leave me alone, or you'll wish you had!' Then I walked away. I drove my rental car back home."

Zita let it all sink in. Judas being involved sounded possible, but they'd need enough proof to haul him in, if they could find him. "Hold on," she told Shannon. Then she relayed the information to Hunter on the radio.

"The guy acted suspicious when I interviewed him. He clammed up in a hurry. I'll head back to his store and see what transpires." Then he added, "Make sure Shannon stays clear. She needs to leave this to us. Take her home and tell her our deputies will make sure she doesn't leave the premises. Make it clear that her interference may endanger her children, especially Charles. Over and out."

Shannon nodded. "I heard what he said. I'm sorry I got involved. I just feel so helpless. Okay, I'll go home with Karla and stay put. I promise."

Zita didn't tell the FBI agents, but she had no confidence in Shannon's promise; that woman was hell bent on doing as she pleased.

Chapter 12

Amidst all of the confusion and searching, deputies still had their days off. Zita welcomed hers the following day, even though it would be a busman's type holiday. She'd be working, but on a clue she wanted to pursue. It was connected to Shannon's case and she hoped it would provide pertinent information.

The night before it suddenly struck her that there might be a connection with this case in the song *Bad News Blues.* Shannon said Judas referred to another song in his phone threat yesterday. Also, in the note she'd retrieved from the bottle, Goldie said Wylie knew the lyrics.

Maybe he didn't know them all. In any event, Zita was going to spend her day off searching bottle trees to find them for herself. Maybe she could cut the sails out from under Judas' wings.

First, she went back to check any bottles she'd missed at Mama Cheche's. Nobody was around, not even another snake. It didn't take long to see that the remaining bottles were empty. Next, she went to the

Tollar Plantation, parked her car in a dense clump of trees and sneaked behind the cotton gin. Only one deputy was guarding the house and he was sitting on the back steps. Zita checked each bottle but with no results.

She got back to her car and sat there a moment trying to think of where else to look, and where bottle trees might have been so many decades ago. A line struck her *Just read the headlines.* There was a bottle tree behind the old newspaper office, now deserted. *Nobody's there; I'll check it out.*

The old Bottle Tree was covered with vines. Zita hoped it wasn't poison ivy. No matter, she pulled them off and examined the bottles one by one. In the tenth one, an old milk bottle, she spotted a piece of paper. It was near the top, so she could reach a corner of the paper to pull it free. It tore but only on a corner. She sat on the ground and read words scribbled on top of the sheet:

Wylie's been after me to give him the rest of the words of my song. He's mad because I won't do it. He says I owe him money for using his car but I don't. I paid him for that and he charged me more than he said he would. I don't put anything past him.

Oh, Eleanor, my wife, I hope you got my message from Mama Cheche about where to find these notes. Maybe you can get my song published. I don't think I'll be around to do it myself.

Here's the last few verses:

I'm in the blues grip

And I can't shake them free

It's a one-way trip

And the river's got me.

Bad News Blues

I got no lifeline

These blues are an anchor

Drag me down one last time.

Bad News Blues

And I ain't gonna lie

These blues will be with me

'Til the day that I die.

Bad News Blues.

After returning to her office, Zita reread the note and the lyrics. Evidently, Mama Cheche didn't give the message to Eleanor. Maybe by the time she saw Goldie's wife again, she'd forgotten it. But Mama had a good memory. She may have passed on the message and Eleanor couldn't find the notes. It was history, so who knew?

The only person who might cast some light on this wasn't likely to cooperate. Judas Martin's interest in this was for himself and what he could gain. It seemed he would resort to anything to succeed. That wasn't going to stop Zita from approaching him.

She left her office to find Hunter and tell him she was checking on some things. When she couldn't locate him, she returned to her office to see him walking into it.

"Are you looking for me, Zita?" he asked.

She placed her purse on top of the note of Goldie's and nodded. *He just got here. I don't think he saw them.* After she told him she was working on her day off, she took the paper home and put it in the same secure spot with the other half of the song.

Dressed in her uniform to look official, she drove to the Get-'n-Go store to question Judas. She strutted inside and waited until he said, "Can I help you?"

"I hope so." She pointed to her badge pinned to her uniform. "I'm Deputy Rocconi and I'm following up on an incident here a few days ago."

He spoke in an unusually loud tone, "Oh, yeah, Deputy. You mean the one with the two women and a boy. I already talked to the sheriff, and the FBI. I told them I didn't know a damn thing. You're wasting your time, and mine." His eyes darted to the storage room in back with an exit leading outside. Zita thought she heard a door open and she tried to push past Judas who blocked the way.

"Let me by!" She manipulated her way around him.

If anyone was there, they'd managed to get lost in the trees and bushes in record time. Zita returned to the store. "Was anyone back there? Tell me the truth!"

"Not that I know of. I usually keep it locked but I just put out the garbage."

"Can you tell me about what happened when the women were here? Did the one in control pass you a note?'

Judas poked out his lip. "No. Like I told the FBI and Sheriff Hunter, I don't know anything. I don't need to repeat it." He poked out his bottom lip.

"I understand you've been harassing Ms. Brown about a recording of Goldie Parsons.

"It's not hers. It should be mine. She just needs to admit it."

"We'll have to check into that. One more thing: What's this you were telling her about another song of Goldie's?" She left it wide open to see how he'd react.

"Whatever songs Goldie wrote should have belonged to my great-grandfather. He and Goldie wrote them together and Wylie Martin never got a dime. He was gypped. So, I'm due his share as his only living descendant."

"How can you prove this?"

Judas bobbed his head up and down. "I got a copy of most of the verses, in my ancestor's handwriting."

"That's not conclusive. He could have copied what Goldie wrote."

A customer entered the store and that was Zita's cue to leave. She wasn't going to get anything else from Judas. But she did get his admission that he was the one who made that phone call to Shannon demanding money. That was a start.

On the drive home, after checking to see if they had any word from Frederica about releasing Charles and all reports were negative, she stopped for a cup of coffee at the Delta Diner. Levenia, the proprietress who knew everything that went on in Cleveland, came over with hands propped on her hips. "Why are you in uniform, Zita, it's your day off, isn't it?"

"Just doing a little snooping on the side." She didn't elaborate.

"Any news on little Charles?"

"Not yet, I'm sad to say."

"You think that new guy at the store out on the highway has anything to do with it? I heard he's old Wylie Martin's great-grandson and wants in on Goldie's fame and fortune."

"We don't know how, or if, he fits in yet. How about a cup of coffee?"

"Coming up." When she brought it right back, she said, "Tell Hunter this case is keeping him too busy. Haven't seen much of him since it started. Enjoy your coffee."

Zita didn't think it wise to confide in Levenia. Still, she needed someone to talk to, someone to buff information off of. A confidant, but who? Her limited list had only a few names: Hunter, not a good possibility because she'd gone against his advice by finding the bottle tree notes. Chan she wasn't close to, Besides, he was a follower rather than a leader. Daryl, who'd been working on another case, and the only one left to consider, had a personal interest in the case, and its revelation would satisfy her curiosity. Also, his intelligence made him good at his job and she could trust him. He wouldn't reveal anything confidential. Now all she had to hope for was that he'd agree to be her cohort. *No, no, no. I'm not thinking straight. It's time to tell Hunter. The link with the song may provide the missing pieces to the puzzle.*

A distraction took her mind off of that subject for a while. As Zita drove to a different part of Cleveland and passed by Mama Cheche's, her car sputtered and stalled. She checked the gas gauge. It registered half full. She started the car again and it ran smoothly, but she felt an urge to park and look inside, so she pulled into the driveway. When she got out of the car a chill overcame her. Memories of past visits flashed through her brain the second her feet hit the porch steps–The bullet in the porch ceiling, the interviews with Mama, Goldie's body washing ashore after sixty years, and the unveiling of the case in discovering the murderer's identity.

She looked in the window at the kitchen table and her entire body shook. On its center, the Mojo stone occupied its rightful place. She blinked, and it was gone. So was the table. The room had no furniture. A vision, or what? *Call Tippiny* echoed in her brain.

Zita left, taking the steps two at a time. She wondered what all this meant. Seeing the Mojo stone told her it was at work, maybe in rescuing Charles. But why should she phone Tippiny? Mama's daughter had no biological relationship to Goldie. But she was a lawyer and a friend of Shannon's. Still, She couldn't determine a connection. What did that message mean? She aimed to find out.

Not wanting to be distracted by road issues, Zita waited until she got home to call Tippiny. She used her cell phone and set her recorder. But Tippiny wasn't in her office, so she left a message asking her to call back.

An hour of agonizing over how she'd justify the call finally led to one idea. Zita knew Tippiny had reservations about the Mojo, so speaking of her "vision" might turn Tippiny off. The best she could come up with was to ask what Tippiny remembered about Wylie Martin and his connection with Goldie. That approach might work to open the door.

It did more than open the door. It opened a floodgate.

Chapter 13

Zita, I can't believe you called me this morning," Tippiny said when Zita answered her phone. "Calling *you* was the first thing on my list today. You sure you don't have the Mojo?"

Zita chuckled. "Nope, not with my Italian blood, but I may be part gypsy."

"Okay. Enough of the ethnic stuff. You've called me, so you go first."

"I guess you've heard about our kidnapping case." She didn't wait for a reply. It had made the national news. "Now we have a new person of interest. It's Judas Martin, Wylie Martin's grandson."

"What! You're calling about Wylie and Judas! You won't believe this, but that's exactly why I was going to call you. I've been researching for a precedent for another case, and I ran across a file on Judas. He's been in trouble big time. He has a connection with a gang like the mafia and they protect him. He's been arrested and tried but never convicted. I read his entire history. He inherited bad genes. His father got killed in a bar fight shortly after

Judas was born. His mother disappeared and Grandpa Wylie raised him. Bad influence according to Mama."

"Give me the whole story."

"Will do. Keep in mind this is from my memory as a child. It's also third hand. Mama said Goldie told her Wylie introduced him to a promoter for singers named Tunstall, and he got the gig for Goldie in Memphis. A Mr. Lomax made the recording that became so famous. Goldie trusted Lomax but he suspected Wylie and Tunstall were in cahoots. Nobody knows, but they had a falling out, probably over that issue."

"I have heard something about that but go ahead."

"The up-shoot was that Goldie went missing and Eleanor left Cleveland. That paved the path for Wylie and Tunstall to reap the benefits from Goldie's record. Nobody interfered. No telling how much money those two made from it. Tunstall made a fair share honestly. Wylie got all he could get, any way he could finagle it. Lucky for them, it wasn't exactly illegal, but it was unethical. If they'd tried, they could've found Eleanor. It sure would've made her life easier."

"How about Judas?"

"Judas learned well. He was in trouble before he got into his teens. They caught him with a gang of older boys breaking into a house that belonged to an FBI agent. It was an initiation. He did spend a few months in a juvenile facility, but it didn't go on his permanent record."

"Then how did you know about it?"

"I can't tell you that. Let's just say I did a little digging. That usually stirs up some dirt, and it did. It brings me to my reason for calling you. Judas is Frederica's drug dealer. Has been for a year, at least."

"You know about Frederica? How? They haven't released her name."

"Ah-hmm." Tippiny cleared her throat. "We lawyers have our methods."

Good God. Zita pressed fingers against her temple. *Did just looking at the Mojo stone bring this result? Is it really magic? Or a coincidence? Well, in any event, now I know why I was inspired to call Tippiny.*

"Are you there?" Tippiny asked because of the pause.

"I am. I'm just stunned. Hey, Girl, all the information you just told me makes me wonder. It's uncanny that we both were going to call each other about the same subject/people–Wylie and Judas, and even Frederica. How could that be? You said you don't have the Mojo, but this sure sounds like you do." She stopped without telling Tippiny about seeing the stone; that would be taking things too far.

"Oh, no. I'm based in reality and more inclined to believe in coincidence, or fate's plans, being carried out. It could be by a force beyond our ability to recognize." She took a deep breath. "Many would say it's God's will in action. I don't know. Look, I've got to go. I'm due in court for a big trial. Call me back if you have any questions, and please keep me posted. I hope you can rescue that little boy and bring the kidnappers to justice. They deserve a long sentence."

The word *kidnappers* in the plural form stressed that Tippiny put Judas in the mix. It slanted the case to a new angle. With so much to tell Hunter, she didn't know where to start. She went to bed but couldn't go to sleep. Tossing and turning along with thoughts in her brain doing the same, she pictured a scenario. If she told Hunter about the bottle trees and showed him the notes first, and his temper flared, maybe following up with the connection between Frederica and Judas would calm him down.

Confidence said he wouldn't fire her. Disobeying his orders not to pursue hunting for those notes was done on her own time. In addition, it produced worthwhile information. How could he fault her for that? Calling Tippiny was equally beneficial. The next step would be to follow up. Now they probably had enough evidence to haul Judas to the station. Maybe they could break him down. She bet he was Frederica's accomplice who drove the car away after retrieving the ransom money. Ammunition, they had. Proof still hung in the balance.

Zita hopped out of bed. *Oh, dear God, I think I forgot to turn on my recorder when I was on the phone with Tippiny.* She checked it and discovered she was right. *Hell, how'd I do that? Now, I've got to tell it all. I'd better make some notes while the conversation is still in my mind.* Opening her laptop, she sat on her bed and typed. Then she got up and printed the two pages of results. Flopping back into bed she rested her head on her pillow, soft and comfortable. But thoughts disturbed her efforts to go to sleep. So she reassured herself about her boss's reaction. *Hunter trusts me; he will believe me.* Second thoughts invaded her confidence. *Won't he?*

Zita awoke at five a.m., an hour before her alarm jingled. She made strong coffee and poured cornflakes into a bowl with milk on top. Consumed with facing her first task of the day, a confrontation anticipated with Hunter, she hardly realized what she was eating and drinking. The chore challenged her like nothing had done since the Rapier Fogg case. She pushed it out of her mind and concentrated on the present. Diplomacy held the key to the proper approach. But diplomatic words wouldn't surface in her brain. She feared blurting everything out and making a mess of it, making it all more surreptitious than it was.

Daryl and his polished demeanor came to mind. Maybe she could relay everything to him and let him tell the story to Hunter. Nope. A third person shouldn't be involved. That smacked of guilt. And Zita didn't feel guilty because her endeavors had resulted in discovery. The issue and the obligation fell right back into her lap. *I made the mess; I've got to clean it up.*

Wearing a little more make-up than usual and sporting Chanel Number 5 perfume along with a broad smile, Zita went straight to Hunter's office when entering the station at eight a.m. sharp. He looked up from his desk. Studying her for a second, he leaned back in his chair. "Well, you look bright and cheery this morning."

"Thank you." She nodded. "I hope you'll think my reports are as appealing."

Hunter narrowed his eyes. "Sit down and shoot, and we'll see."

Zita sat but squirmed in her chair. "I hope you won't *shoot* me." Zita started out fine, but each time Hunter frowned at her story, she stumbled and then blurted out the next sentence or two. When she'd finished both reports, though, her boss laughed aloud.

Seeing her puzzled face, he explained why he found them humorous. "You didn't guard the notes from the first bottle quite enough. I was in your office before you got there the other day. I saw the song lyrics and figured out how you got them. Daryl hinted at some other paper you had related to Goldie, but he only saw a line or two of lyrics. So, I really didn't know about the second one until you told me just now."

He leaned forward. "You don't give me enough credit, Zita." He pulled out a file marked *Martin, Wylie and Judas–Frederica.* "Almost everything you told me is in these papers. I read them all last night. We'll go search again. Hell, it's possible that Frederica has Charles holed up in the woods there since it appears she and Judas are in this together. We have enough to bring him in now. "

She didn't ask how he got that information. She'd get the same answer Tippiny gave her. Hanging her head, Zita walked out of her boss' office, after glancing back at the broad grin on his face. It would fade though when the business of finding Charles and Frederica started again. Relief surfaced that she didn't have to worry about those reports anymore. That was settled. Better yet, hope raised its head. Maybe after three days they'd find Charles safe and capture the culprits.

But the deputies had searched the fields behind the store along with the two FBI agents. Could all of them have missed her car parked there? She could have moved it around and kept one step ahead of them if Judas warned her they were coming. Despite what she wanted to believe would happen–a rescue and an arrest–Zita had to allow for a five-letter word hanging over their heads– MAYBE!

Chapter 14

When they resumed their search, Hunter drove. In the seat beside him Zita had her arms folded and her eyes focused straight ahead. The silence got to him. "You mad at me? C'mon, now. Don't be angry because I upstaged you. It's my job. I *am* the sheriff and I'm supposed to be on top of things."

Zita turned her head and stared at him. "We've always *shared* information, *Sheriff.*"

He looked back at her. "Now wait a minute, *Deputy*. That boat floats both ways. You didn't share the bottle tree-find with me."

She stiffened her shoulders. "Of course I didn't. You'd have bawled me out, maybe even put me on report because I disobeyed your orders–even though I did it on my own time–mostly."

Zita glistened when she got angry. Fire brought out the green in her eyes. Instead of countering, Hunter said, "No, I wouldn't have done either one. I might have fussed a bit, but that's all. I thought you considered me fair and trusted me, Zita. It's how I feel about you." He leaned a little to her side. "I thought we were, er, close."

Her expression changed. She blushed, sighed, and moistened her lips. "If that's a left-handed apology, I accept. But…"

"No *buts* about it. Let's stop at the Diner for coffee. I've talked to Levenia, but I didn't find anything new. Maybe together we can dig something out of her. She's Miss Information. The agents don't know a lot about her. Maybe we'll beat them and get a heads up on Judas from her. Who knows?"

As soon as they sat down, Dewayne popped over and spoke to them. "'Mornin' folks. Ain't seen nothin' or nobody, not even Judas. I usually get my coffee at Get 'n Go in the mornin' but he wuzn't open today. So, I hitched a ride here."

"What time does he usually open?" Hunter asked.

"Seven, but he'll let me in 'fore then, if he's there early." He scratched his head. "Wonder if he's sick."

Hunter's thoughts stirred. Anyone at a convenience store calls in sick long before opening time, or they get fired. He didn't think Judas would want to be fired, but he might just quit. This could be urgent. He pushed back his chair and called out, "Can't wait for coffee, Levenia." Donning his cap, he headed for the door with Zita right behind him.

"Judas is teamed up with Frederica. They could have become frightened and split. Or they may have just decided to move on. Maybe they've found a better patsy. What I'm worried about is Charles." Hunter used his siren and stepped on the gas until the speedometer reached sixty-five miles per hour as it bumped along on the dirt highway. At the store, he pulled up to a stop. His was the only car in the parking area.

Lights lit the store's interior, indicating it was open. "Good grief, I feel foolish. I shouldn't have taken Dewayne at his word. He's not reliable. Everything looks normal." He got out of the car. "Let's go in, Zita. I don't see any customers. We may as well check it out as long as we made the trip here. Maybe we can dig something out of irascible Judas or maybe he'll drop a clue."

When Hunter pushed against the door, he came up against resistance. "Time to replace these doors with automatic ones," he told Zita.

"This store's never been updated. That won't happen unless some driver crashes into this door and tears it down."

He shoved harder, forcing it open and it stayed that way. "I'll shut it on the way out." Nobody appeared behind the counter, so he called out, "Judas, it's Sheriff Harley. Are you here?"

No answer. He and Zita walked down the aisles but didn't see anybody. Then they went into the back room, turned on the light, and found the door locked. No coffee perked on the counter and the cash register was closed. Hunter leaned over the counter and tried it, but it was also locked.

"Let's check outside. Somebody had a key to get in. They may still be here somewhere. Odd–looks like they didn't take anything." Zita exited and Hunter reached for the entrance door to pull it open in case it was stuck and not locked. What he faced was the worst scenario he'd ever encountered. Even as a seasoned policeman, his knees shook as he gasped. "God Damn!"

Chapter 15

The expression of profanity from a man who used it rarely shocked Zita. She stepped back but realized she had to face whatever lay before her. Mustering strength, she looked beyond Hunter, who still stood in the door. A man's head and one limb separated from his body shocked her. He was decapitated and his right arm had been severed, but the rest of the body was still intact. Blood soaked the corpse's clothing and was splattered all over the floor and the walls. Making the Sign of the Cross, she ran outside and threw up. Then she returned pale-faced to tell Hunter, "I've seen a lot on this job, but nothing to equal this. That's Judas. No man deserves to die like this. Oh, dear God, who could've done this?"

"Only a person with animal instincts." He touched the arm still attached to the body. "Body's still warm. He hasn't been dead long." He looked down at the wide-open eyes full of terror. The attached hand grasped a set of keys. On his phone, Hunter notified the FBI agents, explained the situation, called for an ambulance, and for the medical examiner. He also told Jean Guidry. "Get dogs from Jackson ASAP. I'll take off the sleeve of his shirt for the dogs to track with." Hanging up, he took the entire sleeve from the severed arm.

Turning to Zita, he said, "That trip from Jackson will take four hours. If you know of any dogs here, call and try to get them. Tell them we'll pay well." Walking out the door, he added, "Get something to cover the body and you stay here. I'm going to start a search." He didn't have to tell her he'd be looking for Charles.

Zita found a large piece of green plastic in the back room to cover the body and its scattered parts. She kept her head turned while she did so. Diverting her attention, she thought of a couple of bloodhounds a local man owned. They'd been in his car barking at her when she issued him a speeding ticket a couple of weeks ago. She remembered his name, so she called the station and asked Chan to get in touch with Donald Gable. Something was better than nothing.

A bevy of deputies pulled up in front of the store in less than ten minutes. Officers hopped out and converged upon Zita. She gave them orders to look for anyone, or anything, suspicious, especially for Charles. She didn't have to try to describe him; they all already knew who he was and what he looked like. Leaving her alone with the body, they joined Hunter's search.

Spreading out, they looked in all directions. No dwellings were nearby but they searched barns, reporting back on radios that nothing showed up. None of them saw either a person or a car until someone found tire tracks. Zita heard on the radio that all of the deputies, and Sheriff Hunter, rushed to the scene.

Back at the store, the ME arrived and made his appraisal, reinforcing Hunter's assumption that the murdered man hadn't been dead for more than an hour. He said the murder weapon may have been a machete due to the type and size of the wounds. But the only weapon found was a large hunting knife strapped to his side, attached to his belt. He had no chance to draw it, much less use it for defense. Zita stood silent while the body and its parts were gathered up, bagged, and put into an ambulance to be taken to the morgue.

Once again alone, Zita felt faint. She made her way to the patrol car chiding herself for weakness, but she had to sit down and regather her sanity. The scene she'd just witnessed embedded itself in her brain. She could see the dismembered man, the blood, and despite trying to erase it, it intensified. She pictured a person making the attack, hitting him first with a hammer then with a machete–chopping off Judas' head, and his arm. The horrible scenario made her shake from head to toe. Judas had a name. His agony permeated Zita's being. He became a person to be pitied, not the criminal he was.

"We got something, but not much. They're coming to check out those tire tracks. I bet they're from the stolen car." Hunter's words returned Zita to reality. He looked at her. "Damn! You look like you're about to pass out. Lean your seat back and lie down. I'm taking you home."

She shook her head. "No, I'll be alright, Hunter. I'm just trying to clear my head. Give me a moment."

"Nope, you're going home." He held her hand in his. "Look, this is a huge shock, even for me, a tough old geezer. I'll admit it's the worst thing I've ever seen, too." She eased her seat back, too tired to protest "You're going to take off the rest of the day."

She didn't have the strength to argue any more. At least the horrid scene had moved out. But this was something she'd never forget. The car tracks might provide a lead. Her brain whirled. *But they didn't see a sign of Charles or Frederica, or Hunter would have said so.* More images tried to form in her head. *No, no. I won't even think something like that could happen to Charles.* She shook her head again and moaned.

Hunter looked towards her as he pulled back on the street. "Are you all right, Zita. Do I need to take you to the ER?" A car drove up and a man with a camera hopped out. His badge pinned to his jacket said, *The Bolivar Bullet.* A van followed on his heels. It bore a TV station logo. *How am I going to take care of Zita? I'll need to deal with reporters.*

She came to Hunter's rescue. "I'll be fine. Sorry to be such a damn weakling. I need to be helping you, not hindering your progress. I hate to be a bother."

He reached over and patted her shoulder. "Zita, you're *never* a bother. And you're sure not a weakling. Most women would've passed out cold at that scene. You did fine, believe me."

He left to deal with the media, and he planned to be brief.

His words brightened Zita's spirit and revived her. She'd do as he said. But she wouldn't stay off all day. She'd take a few hours rest and go back to the office. Maybe by then they'd have a line on those car tracks. If they were lucky, they might even have a line on Charles— her biggest hope. The unlikely situation consoled her. She said a prayer that it would come true.

Exhaustion allowed Zita to fall asleep in her lounge chair fully dressed after Hunter pulled out of the driveway. She'd turned on the TV but when the news about Judas flashed on, she switched to another station with a comedy setting. But she only watched it for five minutes. It played on but was drowned out by her dreams. First, she pictured Charles being found in a barn and she and Hunter driving off with him. Next, came a nightmare, a vision of the murder, and she had a hypnic jerk which jolted her awake. Her mind was clearer. What a relief it was to be rid of the horrible scene. She looked at her watch which said 4:15 p.m. No need to go in to work this late. She called Hunter's cell phone to get a report.

No answer. She left a message asking him to call her back, then she got on the radio. He didn't answer. *Something big must be going on. I've got to find out what it is.* Zita smoothed wrinkles from her uniform, gave her hair a quick brush, and refreshed her lipstick. Then she walked to the station to get her car another deputy had driven there. They could tell her where Hunter was, and she'd go find him. No news is good news. Excitement consumed her. Had those tracks led them to the stolen car car, to Frederica, and, most importantly, to Charles?

Then the downside possibility hit her. It was also possible that none of that happened. Things could have morphed into something bad, something about Charles, and Karla, even Shannon. Whatever did occur, she'd soon find out.

Chapter 16

After the bloodhounds arrived with their owner, Hunter gave them a sniff of Judas' shirt sleeve and a shirt of Charles that Shannon gave him. The dog handlers allowed the dogs to roam and sniff around. When they got to the tire tracks the experts established were from the stolen car, they sniffed again on a crumpled piece of duct tape. Hunter looked at Daryl. "Charles has been here, probably the whole time. They may have slept in the car or after closing the store, Judas let them sleep in the back room on the floor and provided them with food. I bet she used the duct tape on Charles."

"From the path of the tire tracks, she drove around the perimeter. I guess that's how she evaded our men when they searched the area. Didn't they see those tracks here before?" Daryl asked.

"Yes, they mentioned them, but they assumed they were from the owner of this land. He comes out often to check his property. It made sense, even if it was a bad assumption."

"Yeah, ha, ha. A teacher once told my class, "Think of the word 'assume' as 'ass - u - me.' We shouldn't 'assume', but we all do it. It's human nature." He looked at Hunter. "So where do we go from here, Boss?"

Hunter rubbed his chin. He ignored Marian and Jean wandering around aimlessly, surprised at their inefficiency. Educated idiots came to mind. He blamed it on their youth and inexperience, glad it kept them out of his way. "Well, if Frederica drove off in a car with Charles, the dogs won't find them. We'll have to do that ourselves somehow. We've also got a murder on our hands. Frederica's a viable suspect. She and Judas could've had a falling out and she wanted revenge. But we have no evidence. I've checked, but no weapons are anywhere around here, unless she buried one somewhere or took it with her."

He didn't add what he was thinking: *Shannon threatened Judas with a gun. She's a possible suspect, too. Oh, hell, it's beyond belief that she could commit a vicious crime like this one. But I can't rule her out.* Hunter did realize that Judas had big time criminal associates and if he double-crossed them, they'd come after him. Their murders were deliberately horrendous to set an example. Not many people dared to cross them. Worse yet, due to high priced, top-notch attorneys, most of them were never brought to justice.

Hunter got out his cell phone. "I'm calling the station to tell them when the dogs get here from Jackson to send them to the Tollar Plantation. Frederica may go there to hole up in the woods nearby. I'll also send some of the dogs to the Crossroads. You go ahead and start looking. We're gonna get her, Daryl."

He called the station and gave them orders. He had to deal with several newspaper and TV reporters who stopped to investigate, but he told them as little as possible in a brief statement directed to all. He didn't want to reveal any more than he had to until he had more information. The killer, or killers, didn't need to be warned.

Then Hunter returned to the gas station for a final check. An oversight; they'd left the ring of keys taken from Judas' hand by the cash register to see if any of them could open it. He picked them up with plastic gloves and found the key that opened it. All the bills were gone but stuck under the tray was a note in a scrawled handwriting.

That bitch has got to get out of my life now. She won't leave on her own. I need your help. There's not enough in this for all of us. If the kid gets loose, he'll tell all, and I ain't going back to jail. When you come in today, I'll give you this to show the boss. He'll take care of her and the kid. Then we can put the pressure on to get that record of Goldie's and sell it for plenty of money. Simpler. Won't have to deal with the law, neither.

He put the keys in a plastic bag along with the note and pocketed them. Then he tried to determine who was who. Judas wrote the note and the bitch surely referred to Frederica. But who was due to "come in today"? It sounded like someone who came into the store every day. And who was the boss he expected to take care of Frederica and Charles? Did that mean he'd kill both? At least he knew now that Frederica and Judas were fighting and that he'd do anything to have her gone, including harm to Charles. But Judas was the one who was dead. What took place? Did the "Boss" come and turn on Judas? Why?

So many questions with no answers. One good thing came of the discovery: Shannon became less of a suspect. However, one of the gang's top-notch attorneys might uncover her accosting Judas. He could beat her up on that. She had a gun and she aimed it at Judas. She was protecting her charge. A mother, even a big sister acting as a mother, had committed murder when the young boy in her care was threatened. It had happened before.

Hunter wondered about the man the note was intended for. Dewayne came to mind. He went to the store daily. Could he have become a messenger? He could get liquor and cigarettes for payment. Did he really go to the store and find it closed that morning, or was that his own alibi? But where would he get a machete? Out of a barn, maybe. It wasn't the machete in his shelter; that one was broken. Besides, it didn't seem like Dewayne's style to kill, especially with those weapons.

A more plausible explanation entered Hunter's mind. Dewayne could have come early and caught the murderer in the act. But who? Another scenario came to mind. Judas' used and sold drugs. If he had held back money from drug sales, the gang leader could have sent a person to take revenge. In either case, Dewayne would've high tailed it away without the murderer seeing him. Then, by acting innocent, he wouldn't be a suspect. He'd probably never admit any involvement and just move on.

Whatever had happened, Hunter hoped Charles didn't witness it. It would have a traumatic effect on that young boy. He'd never be the same again. He didn't want that to happen to any child, much less to one as intelligent as Charles who had a bright future as an adult–if only he could grow up normally. Charles had enough trouble with his mother; he didn't need more.

The next step was to find Dewayne and pick his brain. He probably hitched another ride back to the barn. He hoped he'd be sober enough to interrogate. If he was a little tipsy, though, Hunter might be able to pull a few straws out of the hay. Either way, he had to try.

Dewayne wasn't difficult to find. Hunter went to the barn across the field and the man was in it dead to the world. He shook Dewayne awake. For some reason, he didn't seem drunk, but it took about ten minutes to get him coherent. In slurred speech he answered the sheriff's questions.

"What time was it when you arrived at Judas' store this morning?" Hunter asked.

Dewayne yawned. "A little before seven. I, er, I waited 'bout fifteen minutes, but he didn't show up. Later, I heard on the radio," he patted the one beside him, "what happened. Thas horrible."

"Did you see anybody? Was the door locked?"

"Shore it was locked. Only Judas had the key, lessen some big shot at the office has one. Didn't see nobody else, neither. It was dead around there."

"What happened next?"

"Like I tole ya at the diner, I left."

"You didn't see anybody drive up when you were leaving? You didn't stop anywhere?"

"Nope. Nobody and no car. Wouldn't a seen Judas' car nohow. He usually walks to work. When he does drive, he parks behind the building. And I didn't stop nowhere."

Stepping within inches of Dewayne's face, Hunter said, "You're sure you didn't see Judas get killed? Was somebody striking him with a machete or a sickle? That woman you saw earlier?"

Dewayne stepped back, tripped, and fell backwards. He held crossed arms in front of his chest. "I didn't see nothin'! And I didn't kill Judas. I'm a peaceable man. I never hurt nobody. I'm tellin' you the truth."

Hunter helped him up. "Look, Dewayne. I'm not accusing you of anything. But if you saw something, you'd be smart to tell me now. I got a note from the cash register and it mentioned a messenger who came into the store often. Tell me, is that you?" He grabbed Dewayne's arm and pulled him close. Their noses almost touched.

"No, no, not me. I don't know whatcha talkin' 'bout. Lemme go." He tried to pull free but Hunter held onto him.

"I don't believe you. We're going to the station and you can spend the night in jail. The charge is vagrancy. Maybe after a good night's sleep, when you're sober, I can wring the truth out of you." He took Dewayne to the station and locked him in a cell. Dewayne's shifty eyes made Hunter think he was hiding something. Tomorrow, with a little digging, he might find out what.

The dogs from Jackson didn't find a clue at Tollar Plantation or at the Crossroads. They sniffed at items in Charles' bedroom but that's all. After a few hours, they sent them to a kennel to try again in the morning. While he was there, Hunter decided to question Shannon.

"Now this is just routine, Shannon. Normal procedure in a murder case. I have to ask you where you were between six and eight a.m. this morning?"

"I was here with Karla." She glared at him. "Surely you can't think I had anything to do with Judas' murder."

"As I said, it's just routine. You did threaten Judas with a gun. You told me that. Did Karla see you during that time?"

"She was asleep. Anyhow, she wouldn't know about time. You know that, Hunter."

"Kids sometimes pay attention when you least expect it. Was anyone else here?"

"That's an unnecessary question when you know your deputy was on guard. Why don't you ask him? He'd have known if I left. He's a good witness."

"He might not if you slipped out the back way. Once again, I don't really suspect you."

"Thank you for that." She squinted. "I heard the killer used a machete or a sickle. You don't really think I could…" She shuddered. "I've seen a sickle, but I've never held one and I've never even seen a machete. I'm not strong enough to behead a man. Good Lord, I don't think I could shoot someone in self-defense, much less hack them to death."

"I don't think you could either, Shannon. Sorry to put you through that, but I have to ask. It's my job. Anyhow, as you know as an attorney, another defense lawyer could put you on the witness stand and blast these same questions at you. It's best to be prepared." He sighed. "Take it easy and take care of Karla. We're trying as hard as we can to catch up with Frederica and get Charles back to you." He tipped his hat and left. *She's telling the truth. She does love those kids and a woman like that isn't likely to be a killer. If she were, her goal would've been to kill their no-good mother, not Judas. I'll move on.*

Now that her partner was dead, Hunter thought Frederica would have less of a buffer and she'd be easier to locate. He hadn't known about Judas' car until Dewayne mentioned it. She could've taken it and left the stolen car somewhere to throw them off. Again, he tried to fit into her shoes. If she committed the murder, she'd probably run and leave the area, taking Charles with her.

He didn't want to consider that possibility. If she didn't, she'd stay around, hold her young hostage captive, and outwait them. By outwitting them as she'd done in the past, she may end up getting the prize record. The police couldn't stop Shannon from turning it over to her, and they probably couldn't talk her out of it. Once Shannon made up her mind, that was it. She could be a stubborn woman.

Hopefully, things wouldn't come to that. The best scenario was that the gang committed the murder and Frederica was indirectly part of it. Maybe she knew about it but that was the extent of her involvement. Hunter couldn't fool himself. In his heart, he felt sure Frederica was not only a cohort of Judas but that she had a connection with the gang. She may not have committed the killing, but he bet she was in on the twist. Maybe she knew Judas, not her, would be the victim. He tried to unravel all of the *whys* of the case, but he was stuck on the basics. This murder is most foul.

Part of Hunter's speculation came true. Chan called in on his radio to report that the stolen car was spotted behind the barn where Dewayne camped out. When questioned, Dewayne swore up and down that he knew nothing about it. Nobody knew how or when it got there. Hunter returned to the barn and realized the car was hidden by trees and he may have missed seeing it when he was there earlier. He tried again to outthink his nemesis. She could have driven across the dirt road, parked the car, and returned to steal Judas' vehicle with Charles in tow, duct-taped hands and feet.

When she left and where she went were the questions. How long ago? Hunter feared for Charles' life. She wanted him as insurance and a pawn, but if he became a burden, no telling what she'd do. She had a head start, and time was crucial. Hunter kept reminding himself he was dealing with a nut case. A psycho could become violent at any moment. It could have already happened once with Judas; it could happen again with Charles.

Hunter couldn't sit and wait for a crisis. He put on his jacket and hat and headed for his car. He had to outguess this crazy woman somehow. *She has no motherly instincts; she's liable to crack at any time. God help me; I've got to find her before she breaks down and commits another murder. If she didn't kill Judas herself, I'm convinced she was in on it.* He drove off with his siren blasting, knowing only that the Get-'n-Go store would be his first stop. There, he'd look again for clues, clues as to where to go next.

CHAPTER 17

By the time Zita reached the station, she'd become steady on her feet. She'd calmed down some, but she hadn't been able to shake the queasy feeling in her stomach, nor could she rid her brain of images of the gory murder scene. It flashed in and out of her mind.

Daryl had returned to the office for the day and he brought her up to date on the case. She shuddered. "None of this is good. It looks like we're not getting anywhere." She looked around. "I guess those agents are out investigating. Where's Hunter?"

"He's gone back to the scene, hoping to find a missed clue." He shook his head. "This is getting to him, Zita. He's much more worried about Charles than he'll admit."

"So am I."

"We all are, but the Sheriff lets it all fall on his shoulders. No matter what happens, he'll take the blame." He sighed. "I sure hope nothing happens."

A radio sputtered out, "Hunter here. I've found something. Meet me at the Crossroads, pronto. Bring backup and a dog. Over and out."

Daryl and Zita made a dash for the door. In the patrol car, they took the shortest route to their destination, reaching it in record time. Both hopped out of the car and ran to where Hunter stood beside the large road sign.

Hunter held a piece of crinkled up duct tape in his hand. "Look at this." He handed it to Daryl. Zita read it over his shoulder out loud:

King+ Day after tmor. Here.

Save me!

"It was on the base of the road sign. I almost missed it. Finding it was sheer luck." Hunter took a deep breath. "But I can't figure out what it means. Any ideas?" He looked at Zita and then at his deputy.

"Sounds like he knows about a meeting set here," Daryl suggested.

Zita pointed to the words. "But day after *what* tomorrow? It's obviously from Charles, but who knows when he put it here. The time mentioned may have passed."

"No, it didn't get wet in that rain the day before yesterday. I'm glad it cleared up or we would not have any tracks for the dogs to follow. It could've been yesterday afternoon, or this morning. If it's a meeting, it could be today. But what time?" He tapped his toe. "We have to consider this, too. The meeting may have been this morning, a set-up with Frederica and a gang member to kill Judas. That's done, so we may be too late."

"Boss," Daryl spoke up, "what do you think the *King+* means?"

"I don't know, but Charles is smart; he's trying to tell us something." He held up his hand. "Let's get out of here before they see us and run, if they do come back.

We'll call in the troops to patrol the area. I'll let the FBI agents in on this. And the three of us can keep watch, too. We'll also need unmarked cars."

On the way back, Hunter set up the patrol on his radio and they all left for the station. While accessing cars to substitute for police vehicles, Hunter told Zita and Daryl. "I'm musing over that *King+* and you do the same. Sooner or later, one of us will figure it out." He said the words, but he had little hope of that happening. *I wish King could talk. That cat's so smart, I bet he knows the answer.* He snapped his fingers, "I left without feeding King. You go ahead. I'll stop by my house and fill his bowls. I'll contact you when I catch up."

Before Hunter started climbing the stairs up to his apartment, V came rushing out of his shop. "Hold on. I've got something to show you." He stopped running and panted out, "Look at this. King sneaked out and was climbing around on the top of the shelf behind the sculpture and found it in King, Jr.'s ear." He curled his lip. "Can't make much out of it, but maybe you can." He pressed a piece of duct-tape with torn edges into Hunter's hand.

Hunter looked at it. *More tape - must be another note from Charles.* He studied the printed words: *Mama's talking crazy all the time to a man about killing Judas. She hates Judas but he feeds us and lets us stay with him. He's mean like her. He almost broke her arm twisting it. All of them are bad. I heard that man tell Mama they're going..."*

He wrinkled his nose. "Frederica's taken her nuttiness to a new level. Sure makes it sound like she and that guy, whoever he is, murdered Judas." His eyes narrowed. *But if Frederica's arm was injured, it would be difficult for her to wield a machete. She wouldn't have the strength to cut off Judas' head.* He looked at the other side of the tape. "I sure wish Charles could've finished it, or at least dated it."

"A kid probably wouldn't think of dating it." V chuckled. "But King might have."

"Right. Gotta go. Oh, did you put King back upstairs?"

"Sure did, but he didn't want to go. He likes to roam around in my shop."

Hunter knew the cat didn't like to be alone. That's why he often took him to the station. King meowed when he saw Hunter and he went straight to his bowls the minute they were filled. Hunter scratched his ears. "Hey, Boy. You did good to find that tape. We humans probably would never have known it was there." His eyes widened. "Aha! King+--maybe that referred to King, Jr. Ha, I think one mystery is unraveled, and you did it, King." He stooped and stared at the cat. "How about telling me where they were going and when?"

He stood and called in a report about the note for the FBI. Then he left to go to the station. Two or three heads were better than one. His own thoughts were jammed like cars in a freeway parking lot with traffic backed up. He had nowhere to go on his own. Maybe

Zita or Daryl could decipher a hidden meaning in the note. Marian or Jean might even come up with something. Anything was worth a try.

Hunter called Zita and Daryl to his office and shut the door. They might be able to analyze the notes better without distractions. They all reread both and Hunter told him about V saying King produced the second note. "Charles must have put that note in the cat's ear when he took out the envelope. This is the second note. He beat his fist against his chin. "You know what? I'm not convinced I've got it all deciphered. It keeps nagging at me that Charles wouldn't have put down King+. He has a photographic memory. He's seen the name King, Jr. on a placard in front of V's sculpture. He's no ordinary kid. He'd have remembered that and gotten it straight."

"Then what does it mean?" Zita asked.

"I wish I knew. Oh, I'm sure the note at the Crossroads was meant to lead us to the sculpture, but the more I think about it, the more I believe the plus sign suggests another meaning, maybe another King." Hunter shrugged. "Who, or what, I don't know. Do either of you have any ideas?"

Both Zita and Daryl shrugged. Then Daryl spoke up. "I'll check Google and see what comes up. I'll check past records, including Frederica's and Judas's. And that guy, Dewayne. Maybe something will float to the surface. Okay, Boss?"

With a wave of Hunter's hand, Daryl was dismissed.

Zita stared at the note on Hunter's desk. "Too bad he didn't get to finish and let us know where they were going."

"Or it could refer to what they were going to do. We don't know if it was written before or after the murder. He ran a hand through his hair. "If only it had been dated and we knew what tomorrow it meant." He flopped into his chair. "But we don't. I think that time has passed. Judas is dead. I just hope Charles is okay." He slapped his hat on his head. "Let's go patrol the Crossroads area. If he is, this can't drag on. We've got to find that boy before Frederica harms him." He couldn't bring himself to use the words *kills him, too.* Even though he wasn't ordinarily superstitious, he thought saying those words might make them come true.

Hunter and Zita got into a patrol car but didn't get away from the station before their radio blasted out that a patrol car had been stolen from the lot. The report said they couldn't figure out how anyone could even get in the area much less escape with a police car. "Damn it! That's Frederica. I bet on it. Only she would have that kind of nerve." He swerved into the lot and asked questions, but the baffled officer couldn't give him any answers. He didn't see anyone suspicious enter or leave and he didn't see a woman with a child.

What surprised Hunter most was that the car had been gone overnight before anyone realized it was missing. With everyone out hunting for Frederica, all the men thought someone else was using the car. "Frederica has had hours to run around with that car. No telling where she's gone," Hunter told Zita. He popped his knuckles. "She could be in Jackson by now." *If she left here, she may have thrown Charles out on the road somewhere. He could be in bad shape.* "The BOLO is still out on her. We will add the information about the car. We'll check the highway and be sure she didn't dump Charles."

When Zita bowed her head, Hunter knew her thought matched his. He drove on silently saying his own prayer that it wouldn't come true. His goal was to bring Charles back to Shannon safe and sound, but he couldn't deny that with each passing moment that possibility was dwindling.

Chapter 18

Five days after the kidnapping, they were no closer to finding Charles than they'd been on the first day. Plus, they had a brutal murder on their hands with no suspects, only Frederica and an unknown man. The stolen patrol car showed up in a Walmart parking lot in Jackson, but even after a thorough search by the officers that found it, no clues were left behind.

Jean Guidry and Marian Moore searched relentlessly but only came up with things Hunter and Zita already knew. They did find two objects under some boxes in the storage room of the store—a dog collar that would fit a great dane and a broken leash. Upon inspection, they found hair that matched Charles' hair on the collar.

"Oh, my God!" Zita exclaimed upon hearing the news. "She had Charles on a leash."

A picture formed in Hunter's mind—Frederica pulling the leash so tight that it broke Charles' neck. He didn't tell Zita what he was thinking. "Good think the leash broke," was his only remark to her.

With no new information, they could only wait for a note or a phone call. Finally, a message came. The deputy that stayed at Shannon's home called Hunter. Thank goodness they had her phone monitored. It was easy for the deputy to patch Hunter into the call. Frederica's deep voice lit right into instructions:

"You better listen closely. You have one chance to get this right. At seven p.m. today, you and that policewoman, Zita, come to the Crossroads. Bring Karla and an eight-foot ladder. Put ten-thousand cash in the envelope and the record in a bag and tie it to the large tree on the right side of the road. Zita needs to climb to the top of the ladder and put the bag in the tree and then sit at the bottom with Karla. You stay ten feet away in the clearing."

"I'll come with Zita, but I'm not bringing Karla, damn it!"

"Shut up. If you ever want to see Charles again, do what I tell you."

"Let me speak to him or…"

"No. I told you to shut up. I'm giving the orders. This is your last chance. I'll send Charles for the pick-up. When I check it and make sure the money and the record is there, then I'll let him go, but not until then. Oh, don't bring any police except Zita. She better stay at the bottom of that ladder with Karla until Charles reaches her. I have a partner and guns and we'll sure use them if we need to."

She hung up without giving Hunter time to trace the call. He knew it would be a burner phone and it wouldn't be of much use anyhow. He left the station and drove straight to Shannon's house, making the necessary phone calls and plans along the way, hoping to thwart Frederica's typically crazy plans of her own.

Hunter found Shannon leaning over her sink crying and wringing her hands when he let himself in. He nodded at the deputy as he led her to a kitchen table chair and sat beside her. "You take a break and come back in thirty minutes. I'm here." Hunter told him.

"How am I going to get the money, Hunter? It's already two o'clock. What can I do?"

Her eyes pleaded with him. "Please don't tell anyone except Zita. Don't involve the FBI, I'm afraid she'll kill Charles if anything goes wrong." She covered her mouth with both hands. "I can't take Karla there and put her at risk; I just can't."

Hunter's mind whirled. "I have a plan. On my way here, I called a person who's worked with the Cleveland police before, once since I've been here. She's a little person and we can dress her up like Karla and put a bullet proof vest on her. That's at dusk and Frederica's going to be a distance away. I think we can fool her." He took a breath. "Don't worry. I'll scrounge up the money for you. I'll line things up with Zita and she'll pick you up at 6:30. The deputy will stay here with Karla. Okay? Gotta go." He knew it wasn't okay; nothing was. At least he could get the cash from V. When the deputy returned, he headed home to complete the arrangements and hoped for the best.

Time closed in on him. At 6:15 p.m. Hunter made his way to the crossroads. Earlier he met with the six deputies posted in hidden spots near the Crossroads. They all wore camouflage clothing to blend in with the background, were well armed, and had night-vision glasses in case things were delayed until after dark.

Seniority helped Hunter instruct Jean and Marian on proper procedure, although both acted insulted at his patronizing attitude. "We are well-trained, Sheriff. You don't need to tell us what to do." Jean lifted his chin and squared his shoulders.

Marian nodded but didn't use words to reinforce his partner's self-confidence.

"I understand. I just want to be sure you're both safe." Hunter assured them. "Plus, I want your back-up to insure my deputies' safety. We are all in this together. I admit it's as dangerous a situation as any I've ever been in. Even in Dallas."

They all took their posts, behind trees, across the road huddled down in a deep ditch, and in a couple of unmarked cars well-concealed deep in the woods. Hunter stood guard in a low spot as close as he could find and be hidden from sight. His big worry was that someone would sneeze or cough endangering them all. Luckily, by 6:45, cicadas were chirping loud enough to drown out any natural, uncontrollable actions.

At 6:55, Zita pulled up in her patrol car. She got out with the substitute Karla walking beside her. In her hand was a large white bag. She walked over and placed the bag at the base of the Crossroads sign. Shannon exited from the back seat, retrieved the ladder by untying it from the top of the car. Then she carried it to the tree. Without saying a word, Shannon leaned the ladder against the tree and Zita climbed to the top while "Karla" remained at the bottom. Zita tied the bag to the limb of the tree, climbed back down and sat on the ground by Karla.

Doing exactly as she'd been told, Shannon walked unsteadily to a spot about ten feet from the ladder and stood stone still. Hunter didn't make a sound when he let out a sigh. From his position, he saw her body wavering. How long she could stand, he couldn't guess, but he hoped Frederica would show up soon. He didn't think Shannon could last long in her position.

Before the plan could be carried out, a beat-up old truck passed by. The white-haired driver slowed down, stared, and backed up. "Lady," he leaned his head out the truck window and called out, "Whatca doin'?"

Hunter cringed. Then Zita jumped up and yelled at him, "Go away! We're filming a scene for a movie. Get out of here." *Fast thinking, Zita. You're sharp.*

"Okay, okay." The old man scratched his head. "Sorry, I didn't know." He left.

Hunter looked at his watch: 7:07. He hoped this delay wouldn't scare Frederica off. In the shadows, he saw a small figure coming out of the woods. On his radio, he cautioned his men, "Hold your fire. That's probably Charles. Over."

When he reached the clearing, Hunter could recognize Charles, even though his face was partly covered with a filthy, torn cap. It matched his grungy pants and shirt, the same clothes he wore when he was kidnapped. Shannon held out her arms, but he bypassed her, climbed the ladder to get the white bag, retrieved it, climbed back down and walked back into the woods and disappeared from sight. Nobody made a move for about five minutes.

Without warning, a car sped up and screeched to a halt with the motor left running. "Don't shoot. The boy may be in that car," Hunter ordered on his radio.

A woman darted out of the woods and jumped into the back seat. The car scratched off. An unmarked car driven by a deputy bumped its way from its hiding spot and tore after the other car from a concealed area down the road.

Hunter ran to the spot in the woods where Charles disappeared. He looked around the shrubs and growth around the road, but no sign. *Where's Charles?*

He ran to where the woman came from. Nobody there. Then he searched behind some bushes and saw a small body curled up on the ground with its head buried in its lap. It wasn't moving. He stooped close and then saw a hand raise up. "Please don't hit me again, Mama. I did exactly what you said. Please leave me alone."

Hunter's heart hurt. Could this be the arrogant, smart-alecky little boy he'd tolerated in the past? Tamed now, he was subservient, the reverse of this self-confident, precocious boy's former stance. What a change. But it was sad to see a child brought to his knees, and terrified.

"Your mama's gone, Charles." He took the child into his arms and held him close. "You're safe now. Shannon's waiting. I'll take you to her."

Charles dried his tears on his dirty sleeve. "Where's Karla?" He set his mouth. "That wasn't her near the ladder was it? She's not that big."

He hasn't lost his observance ability. That's a good sign. "She's at home with a deputy. Karla's okay, Son. You'll see." They walked to safety together.

When Shannon spotted the two coming out of the woods, she ran toward them as fast as she could. While Zita and the little person folded up the ladder, deputies gathered around and clapped; so did Marian. Jean made a dash for his car to join the chase as did a couple of other deputies.

Shannon grabbed Charles and held him in her arms. he didn't protest. His tears had stopped, and he said in a clear voice. "How could Mama be so mean to me? I'm her son. Even with her twisted arm, she hurt me bad." But he resumed crying louder than ever and his body shook so hard he broke loose from Shannon.

Hunter whispered in Shannon's ear. "I've called an ambulance to take him to the ER. He looks okay, but he needs to be checked." He shook his finger at her. "I'll send the deputy with you to stand guard if they admit Charles. I'll meet you there and interview him. When you go home, stay put in your house. We will keep the deputy you are familiar with there." He bobbed his head. "I've got to give my men orders."

His attention turned to his troops. Next, he shook hands with the little person. "It worked. You did your job well. You may have helped save some lives. Stop by the station tomorrow and pick up your pay. Thank you." He didn't tell her then, but he planned to add $100.00 cash, of his own money, to the check.

When they put Charles in the ambulance and hooked him up to an IV, he was still on a crying jag. Hunter knew it would probably be tomorrow before he could question the boy–maybe even longer.

A crackling sound from his radio turned into an announcement. It was Guidry. "I've caught up with the criminals. They just sped past me on East Sunflower Road. I'm chasing them. Looks like a man driving and a woman next to him in the passenger seat. My police lights are on top of my unmarked car, but they're not heeding it. Still speeding. Wait a minute. They've pulled into the ER entrance to Bolivar Medical Center. Send backup." The car screeched to a stop, then Guidry continued. "We've got them!" His high-pitched voice made the mike squeak. "She's getting out of the car."

For a couple of seconds, there was a dead pause. Then Guidry blurted out, "False alarm. This woman's nine months pregnant. She's bent over like she's in labor, leaning against the car. The man isn't moving. Maybe he's in shock. Cancel the backup. I'll go see if I can help. That woman needs a wheelchair."

Hunter couldn't believe what he heard. The next noise sounded like a scuffle. *Who'd be fighting?* It puzzled him. He hopped into his car and headed for the scene, glad he hadn't canceled the backup. Then it dawned on him that this could be a set up with Frederica. He tried to radio to Guidry but he didn't receive a reply.

By the time he got to the hospital, nobody was near the car in question. Hunter dashed into the ER entrance flashing his badge. A wide-eyed staff member pointed in the direction of the main entrance. "They ran that way," she said. He followed her lead and headed for the lobby.

The receptionist called out, "They shoved a man in the elevator and ran out the front. I saw smoke from the elevator. Hunter went outside just in time to see the car from the ER entrance drive away. He reported it to his deputies. Zita said she was close and would try to intercept that car.

Going back inside, Hunter located the elevators and frantically pushed the button to access it. The door opened and smoke poured out. Guidry lay on the floor. He pulled the agent to his feet. "What happened?" Hunter asked.

Coughing hard, Guidry managed to get out, "The guy knocked me down and ran into the hospital. They threw me in the elevator; The woman held the door open; the man stepped inside and pushed an Up button. Both wore masks. I couldn't see their faces. He got out, tossed in tear gas, and the doors shut."

By then, doctors and nurses converged upon the scene and gave Guidry first aid. He argued, "I'm alright. Let me go." They didn't agree and insisted on making sure he was okay before releasing him.

With no positive reports on the search, Hunter decided he'd be more productive if he could do additional research on Frederica and maybe find out who the man with her was. On his way out of the hospital ER, he picked up a huge pillow laying on the ground by the exit. *Good God! Was that Frederica faking pregnancy?* He didn't have a bag large enough to hold it, so he held it by one corner and tossed it into his car. If it had fingerprints, he didn't want to contaminate them. A small lead, perhaps, but such items often produced results.

Returning to his office, Hunter continued to review the files they had on Frederica, stopping only to grab a sandwich for lunch and skipping supper. All the while, he checked constantly with his deputies in the field. The cars chasing Frederica hadn't caught sight of her. They had no reports of another stolen vehicle, so someone must have given her a car in Jackson. Who, where, why? More questions without answers.

Hunter called the hospital to check on Charles and was told he was still being evaluated. The nurse added that the boy had broken down and was incoherent now. He also talked to Shannon who was close to incoherent herself. "Charles is in bad shape, Hunter. He has a broken rib and his little neck has a dark red band all around it. She must have pulled tight on that leash." She sobbed. "They gave him a sedative and they're taking more tests. I don't know how he's going to come out of this."

Hunter's only consolation was relief that Charles had been freed. One more day may have been the end of this child. His mama's releasing him came as a big surprise. Frederica must have thought he was too much of a drag, a pain, so she got her loot and let him go. He grinned. She evidently didn't know they'd played one trick on her. The record was a fake. It was a cinch she'd be looking for revenge when she discovered she didn't have that valuable treasure. He'd deal with that when the time came.

At nine p.m. his eyes were closing on him as he worked on the computer in his office. Disappointed that nothing new came up, he shut off the computer and went home. Tomorrow was another day. Something was bound to break. His natural optimism and hope surfaced.

Chapter 19

The break came from an unusual source. Hunter had just returned to the office and turned on his computer when Daryl walked in. "Sheriff, I think I have some pertinent information." He pointed to a chair in front of Hunter's desk. "This is going to take some time. Mind if I sit down?"

"Have a seat."

Daryl sat down and folded his arms. "It's complicated. I had a motive for coming to Cleveland. I didn't tell anybody, including you, because I wanted more information first. It's all about Goldie Parsons."

Hunter lifted an eyebrow. "It seems many things in this town connect to him."

"My story does. Let me back up. After Goldie went missing–and now we know he was dead–his mother had another child late in life. So Goldie had a little brother he never knew about. In a flu epidemic, his parents passed away leaving a three-year-old Caleb to be raised as an orphan. Meanwhile, Goldie's record had become famous, but this child didn't know he had any claim to it."

Daryl stared straight ahead. "Skip forward. Caleb grew up in an orphanage. When he was fifteen, he decided to run away. Bad news and good news. Bad news–he got in with the wrong crowd and ended up charged with stealing a car in Jackson. Good news–a young attorney took his case and got him out on bail and tried as a juvenile. The lawyer became his mentor, got him a job at a newspaper, and Caleb's life was headed in the right direction. He eventually worked his way to reporter and then editor. He had one daughter, who graduated from college, was married and expecting her first child."

Drumming his fingers on Hunter's desk, he continued. "When researching one day on his own time, Caleb came across Goldie's name and his fame. It tweaked his curiosity. The upshot was that he discovered his connection to the famous singer. He dug deeper to see how he could help his child profit from the discovery. Proof he needed was missing, but he kept trying for years."

Daryl squared his shoulders. "I am that daughter's child. The 'P' stands for my middle name––Parsons."

Hunter's jaw dropped. "What? Your great-uncle was Goldie's little brother? Unbelievable!" He leaned forward. "Why are you telling me this now?"

"It's about the record. I'm not trying to claim it. I don't need it or the money it would bring, but I want to hear it, to see it. It's my heritage." He looked at Hunter's squinting eyes. "I don't think you gave it to Frederica. Did you?"

Hunter stood, walked around his desk, and clasped Daryl's shoulder. "No, we gave her a fake one. My God, Man, you're full of surprises. I suspected you took this job for a reason, but I'd never have guessed it was this one. So that's your interest in the Parson's case. You've got me wondering what else is going to come out of the woodwork connected to a man who became famous with one record and whose body surfaced from the Sunflower River sixty years after his death. Hells Bells!" He let out a hearty laugh that lasted almost a minute.

"I do have one more thing for you that might be a clue. The gang that Caleb was associated with as a teenager stemmed from Kosciusko, Mississippi, members of the Roi family, renegades way back from generations past. They have a sordid history. You know any French?"

"Only 'oui,' and 'bonjour.'"

"Well, 'roi' means 'king', so they adopted the name Kingsmen. Now they include women, too. I'm pretty sure Frederica has ties with that group."

Hunter made a fist and shook it near Daryl's face. "Wait a minute! Roi is Dewayne's last name and he's from Kosciusko." He puffed out a breath. "Is this the "King+ Charles referred to in his note? This could curl up into a tight little ball, maybe a hangman's knot." He beamed a smile. "I see a light, Daryl. I think you're really on to something."

"I have one more bit of information, Hunter. It's vague, but maybe you can piece it together. It was handed down to me. It's the only thing Caleb Parsons had from his biological family." Pulling a box seven inches long and six inches wide from his pocket, he handed it to the sheriff.

Hunter tried to open the box, but it was tricky. With a smirk, Daryl took it from him and slid the top in a couple of directions and a key fell out. So did a six-inch shell. Holding up the shell, Daryl said, "I'll tell you the story of this first. I don't have a Mojo stone, but I do have this conch shell." He held it up. "Do you know the history of these, Sheriff?"

Hunter shook his head. "Didn't know they had one."

"It's about slavery. It dates way back. When slave ships reached the Caribbean Sea, it was full of conch shells. They used the meat to fatten up their captives, so they'd be worth more money when they sold them. This shell was handed down through the Parsons' family. Ha, we rose up in the world to achieve success. Wouldn't they be surprised?" He put the stone back in his pocket. "I treasure it as a reminder of my roots, and I always keep it with me for good luck."

Picking up the key, Daryl gave it to Hunter. "The story I was told is that a friend of Goldie's mailed this key to his mother. She received it after he went missing. She told friends he'd promised to send her his last copy of his record but was afraid it would be intercepted." He held the key up with the number 161,841.

Hunter shook his head. "That could be a locker in a bus station anywhere. If it's here in Cleveland, those lockers were all replaced decades ago. I don't know what they did with unclaimed contents. Maybe sold them."

"I've checked here and Jackson. They have no record of that number. It was the beginning of World War II. Lots of chaos and confusion. I wonder if he could've meant a footlocker soldiers used." He sighed. "I've been through all of Goldie's files and I didn't see any reference to one."

"Let me ask you something, Daryl. How is this pertinent to the case? I can't come up with a connection."

"I can. I think Frederica is in the Kings' gang with Dewayne and they know about the key and the record. If she can't get that other record from Shannon, she's going to find this one. I'd bet Judas learned about it from his great-grandfather Wylie, but he let it slip and Frederica picked up on it. That's why he was killed." He paused. "I also think they have an idea where the locker is and they just need my key to open it. They may be afraid of damaging the fragile record, so they don't want to chop it open. I'm not sure they know I have a key."

"Probably not. But they're persistent and shrewd enough to figure it out, sooner or later. We just need to stay one step ahead of them." He looked at the box in his hands. "I can secure this in a safe place. I'll put it in the evidence room."

Daryl didn't object. "That's fine. I know where it is."

Together they made a list of possible places that had lockers, then and now. They also tried to figure out who Goldie may have known in the military or how he could have gotten his hands on a soldier's locker. Searching through the old files, they came up with one man's name–Mr. Tunstall. He was no doubt long dead, so the next step would be to see if they could find his descendants and hope they knew their ancestor's history.

Chapter 20

On his own again after the two FBI agents were taken off the case when the kidnap victim was released, Hunter mused over leads and the new information all day long. Where could he look? If Judas Martin knew anything about the locker, he took it to the grave with him. Frederica sure wouldn't reveal any secrets, even if they could find her and bring her in. The only name that offered any possibilities was Tunstall. From reports in the files, it seemed that he was honest. Hunter didn't know when or where, but Tunstall had arranged a way to make another record. Goldie trusted him. It was odd that he fell out of the picture shortly after Goldie cut that last record.

Then it struck him that World War II had broken out then. Many men were drafted; others enlisted in the service immediately. Could Tunstall have been one of them? He brightened up. *That's entirely possible. If that's true, it may simplify our search. There would be a record of his service.* He knew it wouldn't be too easy. He could have joined any branch of the service. Also, that was over seven decades ago. Still, the military kept information.

He'd start with the Army to see if anyone named Tunstall enlisted, or was drafted, in late 1941 or early 1942.

The first base that came to Hunter's mind was Keesler in Biloxi. He looked up. It opened in 1941 as Keesler Army Airfield, named for a World War I Army Lieutenant from the area who was killed in action. It later became Keesler Air Force Base. Google confirmed that servicemen in World War II did have lockers. But when barracks were torn down and replaced, only a few lockers survived, and they went to museums.

Hunter came across that information while searching for Tunstall. He wriggled in his chair. *If Tunstall is the man's first name, I may never find him. If it's his last name, at least he isn't a Jones or a Smith.* After half a day of futile attempts on email, he decided to call on the phone and see if he could have any better luck. He got in touch with the National Personnel Records Center in St. Louis, Missouri. They asked questions he didn't know answers to. *What's the man's first name? Date of birth? Which branch did he enlist in? When? At what recruitment center? Did he survive the war? Was he missing in action, or killed?* All were asked after he told the person on the other end of the phone that all he knew was the name Tunstall, the locker number 1918, and that he had lived in Memphis, TN at the time he would have enlisted, or been drafted.

After requesting to speak to a supervisor the third time, the responder put him on hold. Ten minutes later, he explained to the supervisor that he was a law enforcement officer who needed any information at all because it involved a murder case. The reply, "You have such a small amount of information to work with. Give me time to work on this and I'll call you back," gave Hunter a glimmer of hope.

He was glad he'd also given the sergeant his email because in three hours, something popped up from the St. Louis Center. "Lucky break. We located a Tunstall who enlisted at our recruiting office in Memphis on December 30, 1941. First name Peter. He did basic training at Keesler in Biloxi. Shipped out to the European Theater six months later. Could that be the person you're looking for?"

"It could."

"Sorry to tell you this, but he was killed in action in 1942. I can send you the details."

"No need. Can you just tell me about his survivors? What happened to his belongings? Any contact information would be helpful."

"Okay, Sheriff. I'll sort through this and check the protocol to see what I can release to you, if I find anything."

"How long do you think it will take? We're chasing a murderer here, so time is of the essence."

"I'll give it priority. I can't promise, but maybe I can finish today and overnight it for you tomorrow morning."

"That would be great. Thanks so much." Hunter hung up, leaned back in his chair and exhaled deeply. *Finally, I have something to hang my hope on. Maybe by this time tomorrow, I'll have a clue.* He shook his fist in the air. *Goldie, you've been tormenting me ever since I took this job. Now come through with something worthwhile.* He added aloud, "You hear me?" just as Zita walked into the room.

"You talking to me, Boss?"

He laughed. "No, I'm talking to a ghost–Goldie Parsons." He told her the details. It made clear the reason he was enthusiastic.

She gave him an update on the hunt for Frederica, but none was productive. Reports of sighting the woman led to nothing. "A female even came up to me at the Delta Diner claiming to be Frederica. She was sixty years-old, weighed about 200 pounds and was Hispanic." Zita laughed. "We sent her on her way fast. Hmm, I'll never figure out why people confess to something they didn't do. Attention getters, I guess." She looked at Hunter. "You look beat! It's five-thirty. Why don't you go home?"

Hunter yawned. "I'm leaving. Most places I'd contact are closed. Not much I can do this late in the day." He put on his jacket and his cap. "See you tomorrow bright and early."

At home, Hunter ate cold fried chicken wings and potato salad, washing them down with a room temperature beer. He gave King a piece of the chicken and filled his food bowl. He'd forgotten to put beer in the refrigerator after drinking the last cold one the day before. Halfway through, he dumped the rest of the bottle's contents down the drain. He put a six-pack in to chill for later.

He went to the living room and sat in a chair with his laptop; King curled up at his feet. His determination outweighed his fatigue and he again searched for information far in the past. Considering that Tunstall was an agent, what tools would he have used to promote his clients? The media. No TV then. Radio? Newspapers? He had to have a recording studio to produce records, his own, or somebody else's. How to find it was the big challenge.

Hunter clicked on Google again. It was no surprise to find Sun Studio still in Memphis, but he knew Goldie didn't record there. They didn't open until 1950. He scrolled through the list and checked dates of establishment, finding most started long after Goldie died. Then he came across one that dated back to 1938– Phil's Studio on Union Avenue, a block from Sun Studio where Elvis made early records. He read the detailed history and was elated to discover the name Tunstall among agents who brought performers there when it was new. He called the phone number knowing it was after hours, but he couldn't wait. So he left a message asking for a return call in the morning, stressing its importance.

A cool beer quenched his thirst. Excitement coursed through his body as he anticipated unearthing all the secrets he was seeking. But he didn't want to get his hopes too high. The studio might not have been kept in the family. It could have changed hands many times in the intervening years. Even though they kept the name for goodwill, new owners may know little, or nothing, of its past. *But somebody cared enough to write the history. Will more have been handed down by word-of-mouth?* He gulped down the rest of his drink and tossed the bottle in the trash. He'd had enough of this for tonight. If he didn't get some rest, he wouldn't be able to function tomorrow. He went to bed with King at his heels, but the prospect of vital information from the U.S. Government and Phil's Studio kept him tossing and turning until two a.m.

Chapter 21

Two hours after Hunter arrived at work the next morning, a package arrived. He tore it open with great anticipation. Inside he found a list of clothing, dog tags, and a manila envelope. The note attached said Tunstall had no survivors, so, as he'd requested if anything happened to him, his belongings were sent to Phil's Studio in Memphis. That had been done. It also said, "The pictures in the envelope came later. It seems that somehow they got lost in the shuffle and were never sent to Phil's Studio. We also never discovered what happened to Private Tunstall's footlocker. One hundred sixty-one thousand eighteen hundred and forty-one is an old number, probably from early in World War II."

No details on what happened to the locker. Bet I know, though. Tunstall may have sneaked it out and shipped it to Phil's. Wouldn't surprise me. Soldiers have gotten away with shipping a Jeep home--one part at a time.

Hunter unsealed the envelope hoping to find a record. No such luck. But he did find three old black and white 8 x 10" photos, still intact and not faded. They had to have been done by a professional. He turned one over and looked on the back to find it rubber stamped *Dutton's Studio* with a Memphis address, phone number, and the words–*Fine work for fine customers.* It also had a handwritten number *1562*.

Zita came into his office and he handed her one of the pictures, a wedding couple. "You recognize these folks?"

She took it and gasped. "That's Goldie and Eleanor. Look, you can see his gold tooth! Where in the world did you get it?"

Explaining who sent them, he showed her the other two photos. One showed Goldie sitting on a three-legged stool with his guitar; the other with an unknown man. "You think that could be the agent Tunstall?" Hunter asked.

Zita shrugged. "Don't know. Worse yet, anybody who *would* know is dead."

Hunter grimaced. "Maybe not." He rose from his chair. "This is big, and worth following up on. I'm going to Memphis. I'll go home and throw a few clothes into a bag and be on my way. He hustled past her. "You take charge. If anything comes up on Frederica, let me know." He snapped his fingers. "I'll probably just be gone for a couple of days. I'll get V to feed King; he has a key to my loft, but could you stop by and check on King–just in case? Sometimes V lets him have the run of the place. That damn cat might wander off."

"Sure thing. I'll even play with him. He likes that."

With a hearty handshake and a "Thanks," Hunter left.

At home, he packed a few civilian clothes, but he wore his uniform. He brought food to V for King, saying, "Business trip to Memphis. I should be back in two days, maybe one." Then he threw his things in the car, went to a service station to fill his gas tank, and was on his way. If traffic was light, he could make the hundred-and-fifteen- mile trip in an hour and forty-five minutes. Maybe he could catch somebody at the studio before lunch time.

Thoughts coursing through his mind blocked out the blues music on the car radio until the DJ announced: "Got an oldie for you folks, but one that's kept its popularity for more than half a century, the famous Goldie Parsons' *Reelin' Feelin'*.

Turning up the volume, Hunter hummed to the tune. His mind drifted to what Goldie must have been thinking when he wrote the song. It had such a catchy beat to it, but it was the blues and depressing. It served as a reminder that the artist always knew he was doomed. His short life testified to his fate.

Traveling up U.S. 61, the Great River Road which follows the course of the Mississippi River, he became cognizant of his own fate when an eighteen-wheeler passed him on a curve. It cut sharply in front of Hunter's car to avoid hitting a pick-up truck and missed jamming into Hunter's front fender by a foot. It ran him onto the shoulder but not completely off the highway. A driver behind him blasted his horn as he swerved sideways before Hunter could move forward to keep from being slammed into from the rear.

Pulling back into traffic Hunter took a deep breath. *That could've been the end of me. A truck driver knows better. Why the hell do they take such chances?* Regaining composure, he tried to forget the incident by forcing his thoughts to the people he planned to question in Memphis. He'd checked and knew both companies were still listed as being in business. *It's unlikely that descendants are still running the studios. What if current owners don't know anything about the history or the original owners? This whole trip may be for nothing.* He felt the key in his pocket and glanced at the envelope on the seat beside him. *I'm halfway to Memphis. I don't have anything else to go on. I have to try.*

#

Using GPS, Hunter went straight to Dutton's Studio, but he had to circle the block five times to find a place to park. He put money in the meter for two hours, knowing he'd probably only need an hour at the most. Then he walked a block back to the place he'd seen the sign. The lights were on inside and the door was wide open. He went down a small hallway and reached a reception room. Nobody was at the desk, so he tapped a bell on the counter.

A portly, five-foot eight tall man came out drying his hands. "Morning, er, Sheriff. What can I do for you? I hope there's not a problem." He threw the towel over his shoulder. "Call me Red. I'm an old geezer and I still have a dark room. Been developing some black and white film. It's hard to get that done nowadays, so it helps keep me   afloat."

"That's okay. I understand." Hunter brightened as he reached over to shake the man's hand. "I'm Sheriff Hunter Harley.

He sized up the photographer to be about seventy years old. A rim of faded red hair circled his head with a bald spot in the middle. Stained fingernails testified to years of hands in film developer, fixer, and sepia-toner. It looked promising that he could be a descendant of the original owner.

"Don't worry," Hunter reassured the photographer, "There's no problem. I'm from Cleveland, MS, and I'm looking for some information about some very old photos of a blues singer." He pointed to a 5 x 7 Deardoff camera in a curio cabinet filled with other relics such as a Rolliflex, a Rollicord, and two 35 mm. cameras—a Leica and a Nikon. "You still use any of those or are they just for show?"

"Souvenirs, mostly. I keep them for sentimental reasons. Maybe I'll have a museum someday. They're relics, for sure." Red took out the Deardoff and held it in front of him with both hands. "This one's my baby. Used it for years as did my father before me. From the day the doors opened in 1938 until the late seventies. My dad wasn't quick to change." He shook his head. "Now everything's gone digital and the photography business went down the drain with it. Sad, but true. Cameras on phones did us in. If it wasn't for the film processing and restorations, I couldn't survive. Barely making it anyhow." He scratched his chin. "But you're here on business. What are you looking for exactly?"

Hunter leaned his elbows on the high counter and cupped his face in his hands. "I'm hoping you are sentimental enough to keep negatives from a long time ago." He crinkled his nose. It sounds like you've kept this business in the family. Is your last name Dutton by any chance?"

Red bobbed his head. "Right. I grew up in this business and took over completely when my dad passed. I modernized a bit, but not too much. How'd you guess I might have old negatives? What's the name of the blues singer? Do you have a file number or a date of a sitting?"

Clapping his hands together, Hunter replied, "It was a hopeful guess that you might still be in business and have old negatives. But do they go back to World War II? You know, I'm looking for the person who brought the blues singer here to be photographed in 1941. The file number is 1562. His name was Tunstall."

Red studied himself against the other side of the counter. "Good God! You're talking about Goldie, Goldie Parsons. Tunstall brought him in for publicity photos to help get gigs and he took a wedding photo at the same time. He's the most famous person we ever photographed." He motioned for Hunter to follow him.

In the hallway the first display photo hanging on the wall showed Goldie holding his guitar with a broad smile exposing his gold tooth. It was a tinted 16 x 20" print in a wide gold frame. The frame showed a bit of wear, but Goldie's purple zoot suit hadn't faded. The oils held their color.

"We've used that as a sample forever. I was a kid, but that singer sure impressed me. He sang a song when he was here." He looked at Hunter. ""Reelin' Feelin' it was called. I've never forgotten it. Most likely, I have the negatives in the back room. It would take me a while to find them. I'm running this show by myself. We cross-indexed by date and name. You want copies?"

Hunter pulled photos from his envelope. "I have these. What I'm really looking for is someone connected to Tunstall. They may have information I need."

Red pointed to Goldie's portrait. "He'd have been able to tell you. I remember my dad saying Tunstall was a lot more than Goldie's agent. He mentored the boy, treated him like his own son. Sad that Goldie went missing and Tunstall was killed in the war. If both of them had lived Goldie would have given Elvis a run for his money. I'd bet on it. He did all right after he died though. My dad invested in Goldie and we got some residuals from Tunstall. Quite a bit, I recall. Wish I had some of that coming in now. It sure would help."

Hunter took that to mean that Goldie's trust in Tunstall was well-founded. If he paid Dutton, he no doubt paid Goldie something before Goldie disappeared.

"I'm specifically looking for a locker of Tunstall's. I have a key that may fit it. Ever heard of that?"

"Nope. You could check with the military. They'd have a record."

"I already did. They said Tunstall's locker was missing."

"Tunstall was good friends with the guy who cut the *Reelin' Feelin'* record over at Phil's Studio. Far as I know they're still operating. I think a grandson runs it. You tried them yet?"

"No, but I will. I'll go see what I can find out there." He shook hands again and thanked Red for his time and they swapped business cards.

"It's a pleasure to meet someone who knows about Goldie. I miss the old days. Call me if you have any questions," Red said. "Unfortunately, I have plenty of time to talk."

Chapter 22

Rather than search for a new parking place, Hunter walked the six blocks to Phil's Studio. He passed Sun Studio on the way and saw visitors waiting their turn to explore the famous business where Elvis made a record. It had become a tourist attraction. He might get a ticket when his time on the parking meter ran out, but he was glad he'd left his car behind as he didn't see any parking spaces nearby. As a professional courtesy, he could probably get the fine waived anyhow.

When he reached the correct address for the recording studio, he didn't see a sign, but he went inside anyway. In the reception area there, boxes stacked up five feet high lined the walls. The desk cluttered with papers covered all the space on top except one section for a laptop computer.

He looked for a bell but didn't see one. So he called out, "Anybody home?"

A six-foot slender man came out pushing a dolly with two heavy boxes on it. He stopped to wipe sweat from his forehead. "We're closing, going out of business, but what can I do for you?" His horn-rimmed glasses slipped down on his nose and he adjusted them.

Hunter held out his hand. "I'm Sheriff Hunter Harley from Cleveland and I'm just looking for some information. Are you the owner?"

Shaking hands, the man introduced himself as Bob Phillips. "I'm the owner. But there's not much left to own." He leaned on the handles of the dolly and glanced from one corner to another sad-eyed. "My daddy and my granddaddy made their living here, but things have changed. These agents and promoters today bring in anybody who thinks they can sing. Recordings break your eardrums. Greed. It's all about greed. They make their money on the characters with a one-digit IQ feeding their ego, and they're on their way to the next sucker. Of course, we're guilty, too. We make–made–our money on the recordings, but we weren't guilty of pretending those folks had talent." He shrugged. "It's the way of life."

Then Bob looked at Hunter. "Sorry to go off on a tangent, but I'm sick and tired of feeding people's ego. I want out." He hung his head. "Yet, I really hate to see my family tradition sink into a hole. It's the end of an era."

"Sounds like you have mixed emotions." Hunter studied the man's changing expressions, relief showed through the doomed look on this twenty-something's face. He remembered being that age and some of the trauma in a similar situation. He shook it off. He didn't want to go there. It was too painful. So, he reverted to his purpose for being in this studio.

"Maybe it's a bad time, but I've come here in connection with a case we have in Cleveland. He pointed to his badge. You may be able to help me. You see, I know this studio made a recording for Goldie Parsons way back in 1941."

"Good Lord, I heard that song played just recently. He sure kept his popularity through the years. Kind of like Bing Crosby, but he was a blues singer." He squinted. "Say, didn't you find his body in the Sunflower River a while back?"

Hunter nodded. "We did, and we found a descendant or two. Now there's been a kidnapping and a murder connected with all of this. Did you ever hear of associates of Goldie's, maybe from your grandfather or your father? Do the names Wylie Martin and Tunstall ring any bells?"

Bob plopped into a chair and motioned Hunter to do the same. "Oh, yeah! Martin was as sneaky as they come. I don't know if he ever got into any legal trouble." He shook his finger. "My daddy said Tunstall was as honest as George Washington. I heard all about him over and over. Daddy told me Tunstall was like a father to Goldie. He recognized talent and he really cared about Goldie, like a son, even though he was just a few years older than his protege." He folded his hands in a prayer-like fashion. "We all made money on Goldie's talent. Lots of it, even after Goldie went missing." He shook his head. "Daddy Tunstall would've been so proud of Goldie's success. Too bad he didn't live to see it."

Bob rubbed away the tear under his left eye and looked up. "If you're looking for copies of that record, we don't have any."

It was time to get to the point, but Hunter hedged around the truth. "I checked with the Army and they said they sent Tunstall's belongings to you since your address was the one Goldie listed to get his things if anything happened to him." Keeping true to the palendemic word *mum*, he didn't overstate what he'd discovered.

"Yeah, he didn't have any relatives, and he didn't associate with other promoters. We got a uniform, underwear, a watch, and his dog tags. Nothing worth anything. My dad kept them a while and then donated them to a museum here in Memphis. I don't know which one."

"Before then, when Tunstall was in basic training in Biloxi, did you keep in touch with him? I understand he had some kind of locker that just went missing."

"Ha, ha, ha. Yeah. Tunstall shipped it to us. He found a clever way to get it off the base. Neat trick. Never told us how."

Hunter's eyes widened. "What was in it? Could you open it?"

"Oh, sure. He sent the key." He tapped his temple. "He'd lost Goldie's mother's address, so he wanted my dad to see if he could find out where she lived and send the locker to her. Dad opened it and all he saw were newspapers packed on the worn bottom. He thumbed through them but the only other thing he saw was a picture of Goldie with his guitar, one taken at Dutton's Studio. You been there?"

"I have and I also have copies of that picture." It was time to ask the big question. "Do you still have that locker?"

Bob nodded. "Yeah. Dad never could find Mrs. Parsons, so he kept it for sentimental reasons." He got up. "Let's go see if we can find it. I saw it when cleaning out the other day. I asked Dad for the key, but he's in a nursing home now and couldn't give me a clue where to find it."

It didn't take long to locate the item made out of plywood. It was almost square and smaller than he expected. Hunter just stared at it and waited for Bob to make the next statement. What he hoped for happened.

"Look," Bob offered, "I don't have any use for this. Take it, if you want it. I knew nothing was inside, so I didn't see any need to break the lock." He shook his head. "I sold my recording equipment, Dad's out of it in long-term care, and my wife's expecting our first child, a boy. I'm an engineer by trade. All I want now is to get out of this business and work at something where I can make a decent living." He waved his hand in a circle. "I don't have any place to put all this stuff. Take the locker, or it'll go into the dump with the rest of these things."

Hunter didn't argue. He picked up the locker by one handle. It didn't weigh much and might not be worth anything. Pressing a fifty-dollar bill into Bob's hand along with his business card, he said, "Here, maybe this will help a little."

Bob read the card. "My cards are all gone. But I'll send you an email with my new contact information."

"You have my phone numbers. Just call me if you think of anything."

Hunter sighed as he left the defunct recording studio, glad that Bob hadn't pressed for details of who was kidnapped or murdered. Maybe he'd heard about it on TV, or perhaps his preoccupation with his own problems made him less curious than most people.

Walking the six blocks to his parking place gave Hunter time to mull over things. Now he had the locker and couldn't wait to try the key. If it fit and only revealed old newspapers and one photo, what good was it? Why would Tunstall have bothered to ship it to Phil's Studio? Could they have missed something valuable hidden inside? It struck him that Dutton, Tunstall, and Phil's father had made money on Goldie's talents. Goldie didn't live long enough to reap many benefits, and Eleanor got virtually nothing. All got residuals except Eleanor, who needed money the most, especially when she was raising her daughter. What she inherited from her mother, the Tollar Plantation, came way too late.

Hunter reached his car, unlocked it, and put the locker on the back seat. *Life is so unfair.* He smiled when he looked at his windshield and had no ticket. *Maybe not too unfair. I got one break.* He sat beside the locker and pulled out his key. It fit. As he was told, the photo was face down on the top with stuck-together newspapers stacked under it. He didn't try to pull them apart but just rummaged through their edges. Nothing. He could search more later. He put the object into the trunk. No reason to tempt a robber peering into a car window, no matter how worthless the thief's loot might be.

Feeling hunger pangs, Hunter decided to get a bite to eat. He looked at his watch: 3 p.m. No need to spend the night. He could have a decent meal and drive home by eight p.m. He changed his plans. He knew of a barbeque restaurant he'd heard raves about, the Rendezvous, a famous place. Time to go there. It was behind the Peabody Hotel. So, he found it and a parking spot nearby. The supper crowd hadn't arrived, no line, so he was seated right away. He ordered a rib dinner with potato salad and beans and a beer from the waiter dressed in black pants and a white shirt. *Reminiscent of New Orleans; hope the food is as good as theirs.*

He was pleased to discover that it was. "Your food is superb, even compared to New Orleans," he told the waiter who accepted his generous tip of seven dollars.

The server bowed. "Thank you, Sir. We try our best. Are you from New Orleans?"

"No, I'm from Cleveland, Mississippi. Up here on a case." He pointed behind him. "Say, I have a little time before I leave Memphis. I've heard of the Peabody Ducks at the hotel. Do you know what time they put on the show?"

"Five p.m. In forty minutes. It's worth seeing. Only lasts about half an hour. You'd enjoy it."

"Thanks." Hunter left and headed to the hotel.

The Peabody's lobby was packed. Hunter found a spot behind a short female. He stood behind her and listened to the last chords of a song being played on the piano. A glimpse of a woman walking around the perimeter caught his eye. She looked like Frederica. But he quickly convinced himself he was imagining things.

Diverting his attention back to the action, he wondered how many ducks had swum in the fountain in the center of the room. At 4:45, the Duck Master strutted out in a bright red coat using a cane and began his presentation. As he made his way along the red carpet, he had the attention of the entire audience.

"A couple of men, including Frank Schutt, the General Manager of the Peabody then, started this tradition which dates back to 1930. They played a joke by putting decoy ducks in the fountain. It turned out to be quite a trick, one that people liked. So they used real ducks. I am following in the footsteps of Edward Pembroke who was Duck Master for fifty years, since 1940."

As the ducks ambled around, he continued. "Our ducks are not named. We treat them as wild creatures, not pets. Each team stays three months and then are returned to the farm." He squared his shoulder. But they live like kings while they're here in the Royal Duck Palace on the rooftop of the hotel. It's a marble and glass structure with a fountain. A bronze duck in the middle spits water. It also has a small replica of the hotel and a grassy area the ducks can rest or play on." He held up his index finger. "Another way we honor them is that duck has not been on the Peabody menu since its reopening in 1981. This is the only Chez Philippe Restaurant that doesn't feature it on their menu."

At precisely 5 p.m. the Duck Master motioned to the ducks and they all marched around the fountain. A few children, ages about five to twelve years old, followed in line. Hunter had read somewhere that special packages from the hotel allowed the privilege. It also provided duck cookies, which two children were munching on as they enjoyed the moment of honor in the limelight.

When the act concluded and the Duck Master escorted the ducks into the elevator to return to their palace, Hunter was glad he'd come. The happy event distracted him. At least momentarily, his cares were forgotten. He even managed the temptation to check with Zita as soon as the act was over. He didn't want to ruin his rare, peaceful mood. The seedy side of life in the underworld had been replaced by a few moments of joy and seeing the best in people, instead of the worst. It refreshed his spirit and his faith in humanity.

But the pleasant feeling didn't last long. On the way to his car, half a dozen boys lined up on opposite ends of an alley were throwing rocks at each other. *Better than guns, but not by much.* Hunter pulled out his pistol and stepped forward to intervene, but a police siren stopped him. *Good. They're on the job. I'll let the local police take care of it.* He stuck his gun back in his holster. In the shadows, he waited until the officers had guns aimed at the crowd. One of the boys, a pre-teen, said in a voice that hadn't yet changed, "Aw, officer, we're just havin' a little fun." He held up a rock. "We ain't even aimin' at each other really."

Another from the opposite side chimed in, "Maybe we broke a window; we'll pay for it." He pointed to a couple of rocks on the ground. "Look at the size of those rocks. They shore ain't dangerous weapons."

Hunter didn't wait to see what happened. It wouldn't surprise him if this incident turned violent and the perpetrators pulled out guns. He took the opportunity to get away. As he turned to leave, he stumbled on a pile of stones of various sizes. Ammunition.

Reaching down, he picked up a small stone by the toe of his boot. It made less than a two-inch circle. When he got to a streetlight, he opened his palm and checked it again. *Wait a minute. This is the same size, and color, of the Mojo stone.* He moved out of the light and leaned against an old brick building. *What the hell is going on? Is that stone following me around? It's too close a resemblance to be a coincidence. Good God!* He made a run for his car half a block away. But he stopped before reaching it and slowed to a walk, taking huge steps. *What am I thinking? I don't believe in the Mojo. Why did I run?* He stuffed the stone in his pants' pocket. *I wish Mama Cheche was still around. I want to show this stone to somebody who knows about these things. Hmm, maybe Zita, or Shannon.* He felt it through the cloth of his pants' pocket. *I do wish it could protect me.* Remembering that he was out of the clutches of those endangering him, Hunter smiled. *Right now, I don't need any protection.*

Three steps later, in sight of the car parked close enough to a streetlight to illuminate the front of it, Hunter noticed a paper stuck under his windshield. *Oh, hell. I got a ticket.* He soon discovered that paper was worse than a ticket. He pulled it off and unfolded it to read:

"I followed you here and I went to both studios after you left. Fooled those guys, too. They believed you sent me back to get more information. Ha, ha. They repeated all that they'd told you. I know you got the locker, but I'm not after it. Nothing's in it. I believe that after all these years, they'd have found it if it had anything in it.

But Bob Phillips told me something he didn't think of till you left. Here's a hint–something about Judas. Damned if his name don't fit him. Okay, Mr. Sheriff, that's all I'm gonna say. See if you can figure it out!

GUESS WHO?"

Hunter hopped into his car and got on his phone. First, he called the Memphis Police about the note, and told them to put out a BOLO on Frederica. Then he called his office. Zita answered. "Hey, Boss, I can't wait to hear what you've got?"

He didn't let her say more. After telling her about the note and letting her know he was on his way back to Cleveland, he asked if she had any reports on Frederica. "The note wasn't signed," he said, "but it has to be from her. We don't even know if Dewayne's in this, or what his role is if he is. Anything new on Frederica?"

"I tried to call you. We did get a report that she was sighted in Memphis around that famous Peabody Hotel, about four-thirty p.m. No follow up though."

Hunter thought of the woman he'd seen. Could it have been Frederica? *Damn it! Did I miss my chance to catch her?* He told Zita of his suspicion, but she didn't think he missed any opportunity.

"No, you couldn't have caught her, Hunter. If it was her, she wanted you to see her and had her escape planned. She's trying to torment you. That's what a psychopath does. Don't beat yourself up over this. Look, we'll get her. Oh, I've got another call." She cut off.

He didn't call her back. Her shift was almost over. Nothing he'd learned couldn't wait until tomorrow. Now, all he wanted was to go home and get some rest. He stepped on the gas and eased off when the speedometer read eighty-five. This drive wasn't going to take an hour and three quarters. It couldn't. His eyes were drooping already.

Chapter 23

Although Hunter arrived home completely exhausted, he still couldn't resist checking that locker again. After petting and feeding King, he pulled the key out of his pocket and opened it, as the cat sniffed around its edges. Rummaging through produced no results. He didn't have the will or the energy to remove all of the newspapers, so he stuffed the corners back in place and left it for later. Without undressing, and only removing his shoes, he fell on top of the bed and went to sleep.

The next morning Hunter awoke rested and in a more positive mood. He'd find that woman no matter how long it took or what it took. She was going to get justice–jail time. Eager to resume his search, he didn't make breakfast. He picked up a few doughnuts on the way to the office. Zita would have coffee made. He walked into the station with the bag in hand.

"You brought doughnuts." Zita smiled. "Good, I'm hungry." She handed him a cup of black coffee, and then reached into the bag and grabbed a doughnut with multi-colored sprinkles on top of a layer of chocolate icing. Then she sat down as he walked around to his desk chair munching on a lemon puff.

"I can't wait to hear about your trip. What did you find out? Who did you get to see?" she fired questions between bites and sips of coffee.

He listed all the details of his conversations with Dutton and Phillips and handed her the note. She read it and shrugged. "I don't think she got any new information. She's just trying to push your buttons, get you rattled. It's another one of Frederica's power plays."

Hunter scratched his ear. "I wish you were right, but I don't think so." He reached into his pocket. "One more thing–about those boys fighting…" He handed her the stone he'd picked up at the site. "Here's one of the rocks. Does it look like the Mojo stone to you?"

Zita rubbed it. "It's smooth. Were the other rocks like this? Hmm–damned if it doesn't resemble Mama's old stone." She handed it back.

"Oh, you know how I feel about the Mojo. Even if I didn't see any other polished looking rocks, I don't believe this is any more than a coincidence that I happened to get this one. Let's drop it, okay?" He tossed the rock on his desk. It hit a framed photo of Hunter receiving an award for meritorious service back in Dallas. The picture fell to the floor and broke the glass.

Zita laughed aloud as she retrieved it. "Maybe that's what you get for denying the Mojo, Boss." She held up the frame. "I'll get a new piece of glass and take care of this for you." She turned back when leaving the room and shook a finger at Hunter. "Now don't mess with the Mojo again, if you don't want trouble."

Hunter had to laugh himself as he wadded up a piece of paper and threw it at her back. He missed and had to go pick up the paper off of the floor. He put the paper in a trash basket but it wasn't accompanied by the stone. That went back into his pocket. Even if he didn't believe in it, maybe it would bring him some luck–good luck. *Was that possible? No! Yes. Maybe.*

Good luck didn't materialize. All morning he checked repeatedly for an email or phone call from Bob Phillips and a chance to question him about Frederica's visit and Judas. He suspected she'd told Bob she was an undercover officer with the FBI. And she'd say they took over the case, after letting him know it involved a kidnapping. He could hear her saying, "Don't contact Sheriff Harley; the Cleveland Police are off of this case." The woman had nerve. In Bob's distraught state, he'd probably fallen for her act.

Hunter considered asking the Memphis police to call on Bob and straighten things out, but what valid grounds did he have for such a request? He couldn't prove Frederica talked with Bob. She may have told Bob the case was secretive and not to tell anybody about her visit. Nor could he prove the note left on his windshield was from her. He felt stymied. That woman had him exactly where she wanted him.

The only choice he had was to take a different tack. After lunch, he told Zita, "I'm going to the hospital to try to talk to Charles. He's a bright kid, maybe he can throw some light on this boondoggle of a case."

"Can't hurt," she replied. "He's still in the hospital, but he should be feeling better now; they ought to let you talk to him. Good luck."

Hunter stuck his hand in his pocket and rubbed the stone. For him, a person close to being an agnostic, it was kind of like praying–*If there's anybody up there, please help me.* But he was desperate, so he had to put his faith in something.

Hunter took Highway 8, East to the Bolivar Medical Center. When he reached Charles' room, no guard was on duty. Charles was in bed sleeping and Shannon was sitting in a chair staring into space. She got up and threw herself into the Sheriff's arms. "Oh, Hunter," she cried out, "things have gotten worse. I don't know what's happened but yesterday Charles stopped talking. They've checked a second time for a concussion but that's not it. They don't know what's wrong." She slumped back into a lounge chair and tears flowed down her cheeks.

He handed her a tissue from a box on the bedside table and sat on the edge of the bed. "Where's the guard?"

"He went to lunch."

"He's not supposed to leave his post. I'll see about that when I leave." He looked at the sleeping child. "I don't want to wake him. Tell me what Charles told you about the kidnapping."

Shannon shook her head. "That's just it. When Daryl tried to interview him, he clammed up. He hasn't said much at all, just that he did whatever his mama told him, and she still beat him. He had welts and bruises all over his little body. It's bad, Hunter, bad." She sobbed out the rest. "I can't bear to see him like this. It's awful that it's not getting better; it's getting worse. Now he won't utter a word. When he's awake, his eyes are vacant. I don't know if he recognizes me."

Hunter sank into deep thought. The guard wasn't on duty now. Had he slipped away for a smoke or something during the night? No substitute was on duty, but he was supposed to summon a staff member to take his place when he went to the restroom or would be gone, even for a few minutes. Horror of horrors to suspect had Frederica sneaked in during the night and terrorized Charles into submission of silence. The unfortunate thing was that Hunter had no way to find out.

"Did you spend last night here, Shannon?" he asked.

"No, I had to go home to be with Karla. She's so upset. When I brought her to see Charles, he didn't say a word to her. I guess I left around six p.m. and got back this morning at nine."

Hunter stood. "I need to see if I can get Charles to talk to me. For now, I want to check some things with the staff. I'll stay in the hospital until you call me."

The first person Hunter encountered was the guard who hurried to his post when he saw the sheriff exiting the hospital room. Hunter faced him down. "Why have you left your post unguarded? You're on duty. Nobody's watching this boy's room."

"I, er, I couldn't find anybody and I had to go to the restroom."

"No, you went to lunch."

"Oh, yessir. While I was out, I grabbed a sandwich. It didn't take ten minutes."

Hunter's face reddened and his voice increased several decibels. "You'll be on report. Stay on your post until I order a replacement. You understand?"

A salute acknowledged that he did. But that wasn't the end of the conversation. Hunter then asked, "You were also on duty last night. The boy's had a bad change of condition. I'm not asking *if* you left then, just *when* you left and for how long." He got nose to nose with his deputy. "Tell the truth!'

"I did go out for a smoke, for less than ten minutes. It was late around nine-thirty. Nobody was on the floor. I asked a nurse to take my place, but she must have had an emergency call because when I returned, she was nowhere around." He held up his right hand. "I swear that's the truth, Sheriff." He was shaking and he swallowed hard.

Hunter left without belaboring the point. What was done, was done. But that deputy would have to pay for his neglect, maybe lose a rank. Yet what Charles had lost was much more significant.

At the nurse's station, Hunter inquired about who was on duty last night and he got contact information on three different nurses—one male and two females. All were scheduled for the next shift which began in ten minutes. Hunter decided to wait to interview them. He returned to Charles' room and found both Shannon and the boy fast asleep, so he left.

When one buxom nurse in her fifties said she'd taken the guard's place, she said an emergency drew her from the post. She also said the deputy had been gone twenty minutes. Hunter vowed the man would pay for his lie. The other two nurses weren't involved in the incident, but when asked if any strange person was noticed, the male nurse said he did see a woman he didn't recognize enter Charles' room, but she had on a nurse's uniform, so he thought she might be a new hire.

"We're always short-handed and hiring new nurses, so it didn't mean much to me. Anyhow, I was on my way to the ER - car wreck on the highway - so I couldn't stop to investigate. Didn't see her again."

Hunter cleared his throat. "Okay," he handed all three a card. "If you think of anything else, anything at all might be helpful, call me. Another thing, if you notice the guard away from Charles' door, please let me know. You're nurses; I don't have to tell you how serious this is. A child's life may be at stake."

He left with new knowledge about what had happened. Frederica must have come back from Memphis last night about the same time he did. She had done her worst. She'd intimidated Charles. How she could do this to her own son was beyond his understanding and control. But he did control that deputy and he'd teach that man a lesson, one he wouldn't forget.

He got on his cell phone and ordered two deputies for replacement. Hunter vowed that if they could bring Charles out of this coma-like state, Frederica wasn't going to get near him again to cause a relapse. The boy deserved to have a normal life; one he hadn't had for most of his tender years.

Upon returning to Charles' room, Hunter's hope was to break through this barrier of fear and have the boy open up to him. As smart as Charles was, he could reveal pertinent information, maybe predict Frederica's next move. Then they could capture her. No matter what, she had to be caught and stopped before she committed more crimes, or murder. It was a wonder she didn't just murder her son. Something could've frightened her off last night. If she'd had time, she might have.

Charles was slapping Shannon's hand away from smoothing his unruly hair when Hunter came into the room. "How are you feeling, Charles?" Hunter asked on a cheery note.

Sinking back on the pillow, Charles turned his head toward a wall. No reply.

Hunter edged close to the boy's face and closed his eyes. "Come on, Charles," he said, "talk to me. You know I'm your friend. Tell me what's bothering you." He squared his shoulders and pointed to his badge. "I'm the sheriff. I can fix everything."

A glimmer of recognition surfaced when Charles opened his eyes in narrow slits, but he didn't utter a word. He curled up into a fetal position and reset his mouth in a determined manner.

Pulling up a chair, Hunter whispered. "Okay, would you talk to Zita? Karla?" Hunter clapped and Charles jerked a bit. "I know. What if I bring King here? You'd trust my cat, wouldn't you?" He cast his eyes toward Shannon who nodded. "Yeah, that's what I'll do. I'll go get King. You can have a chat."

Charles' eyes opened wider this time. He didn't speak, but for a second his mouth seemed to form a word. Was it King? It was worth a try to break this awful spell. And that's what it was like—an evil spell cast by Charles' mother. Nodding to Shannon, Hunter patted Charles' shoulder and the boy cringed. No wonder, after all he'd been through and they didn't know half of it. Hunter left to go get his pet. He'd heard of people communicating with animals when they couldn't equate to other humans. Would it work in this case? It was like faith, fate, and the Mojo. Hunter rubbed the stone in his pocket. Who knows?

Chapter 24

In a driving rain and thunderstorm, Hunter stayed on the phone all the way home trying to get permission to bring a cat to Charles' room. After being transferred up the line four times–all the way to the top, with the administrator's permission, Hunter achieved his goal.

King was snoozing on Hunter's recliner. Hunter got his raincoat out of the closet, put it on, and then reached for the cat. He balked and meowed at being disturbed. When put into his crate, he made more racket, sounding off all during the drive to the hospital.

To avoid confrontation, Hunter stopped at the reception desk to explain that he'd cleared bringing in King.

"Nobody's called me," the pert young girl said.

"Check with Mr. Rawlings. I had to go to the top."

She hesitated. "I'm not supposed…"

Hunter interrupted. "Then call his secretary."

She pushed a couple of buttons. "It's voicemail. I can't let you by." She looked toward the elevator at a guard.

Removing his dripping wet raincoat. Hunter pulled out a twenty-dollar bill and showed her his badge. "I'm the sheriff and I assure you I have permission to take my cat to this boy's room for medical purposes. If you call security, I'll pull rank on the guard." He laid the money in front of her on the desk. "Take this for your trouble."

Her bottom lip quivered. "I'm just doing my job, Sheriff." She didn't touch the bill. "Your cat's cute." She cracked a smile. "I like cats."

Hunter nodded. He and the crated cat headed for the elevator. The guard moved aside. Looking back at the receptionist while he waited, he noticed she picked up the twenty-dollar-bill and slip it into her purse. A door opened and Hunter stepped inside. He knew the hustle wasn't over. He'd still have to get past the nurses' station.

That problem didn't occur. No nurses were at the station at the moment. Taking advantage of the opportunity, Hunter hurried down the hall, spoke to the two new guards at Charles' door and darted into the boy's room.

Uh, oh! An aide was placing a meal on the bedside tray. *Another hurdle.* She looked at Hunter, then pointed to the cat. "Is he supposed to be up here?"

With an air of self-assurance, Hunter said, "Yes, we're hoping he'll be able to help Charles." Pointing to the door, he added, "It's fine. You can leave." She adhered to his order.

Shannon had remained silent, but after the girl left, she burst out laughing. "Hunter Harley, is King *really* supposed to be here? Or did you just con that young lady?"

Hunter bowed. "I have permission from the hospital administrator to allow King to be here."

He glanced at Charles propped up on a pillow, staring into space and not even looking at his food. His eyes shifted to the caged cat, but they remained expressionless.

"I see a glimmer of interest," Hunter whispered to Shannon. "This just might work." Opening the cage door, he took King into his arms and scratched his ear. "Do your stuff, Boy. I'm counting on you. You'll get all the treats you want. They're right here waiting for you. Patting his pants' pocket, he felt the Mojo stone. "You can help, too!"

What am I saying? This must be getting to me! He put King on the foot of the bed. In seconds, the cat crawled up close to Charles and rested its head on the boy's chest. Still looking frozen in time, Charles lifted his hand and placed it on the cat's back. King didn't budge. When Charles stroked the cat's back, he purred.

Shannon rose, but Hunter put his finger to his lips and whispered in her ear, "Don't interfere; you might break the spell. Let this play out."

Taking his cue, she sat back down, transfixed with the scene. It didn't last long. A doctor wearing a badge bearing the name *Alton* burst into the room booming out, "How are we doing today, Charles?"

The momentary spell was broken. Charles slumped down and again curled up into a ball, squeezing his eyes shut. Taking the hint, King hopped off of the bed and ran toward Hunter, jumping into his lap.

The doctor stopped in his tracks, looking first at the cat, next at Shannon, and his gaze stopped when he focused on the Sheriff. "What is going on here?" he asked.

"Nothing now." With King in tow, Hunter took the doctor's arm and escorted him to the hall. He explained the experiment and was surprised at the doctor's reply that maybe it would work--he said he'd seen it happen before with a dog.

Apologizing for the disruption, the doctor said, "We've tried everything else with no good results. You may as well try again to let the cat draw Charles out. Please let me know what happens." He handed Hunter his card and was on his way.

Seeing a nurse headed his way, Hunter returned to the room before she spotted the cat. Charles had not budged. With her head hung between her knees,

Shannon didn't look up but stammered, "Oh, dear God, Hunter. Why did that doctor have to come right now? I thought this was going to work. Charles was reacting." She rose up and banged her fist on the bedside tray. It shook. The dinner plate fell to the floor and food splattered everywhere–on the bed covers, on Charles, and on the floor where it cracked into pieces.

Shannon screamed. "Damn it! I've had all that I can take." She reached for the buzzer and called for someone to come clean up the mess.

An orderly entered shortly. "What happened here? Did the boy get angry and use his plate like a Frisbee?" He chuckled at his own joke. Neither Shannon nor Hunter reacted to the attempt at humor, nor did they tell what caused the mess. He took the hint, cleaned up the food, changed the bed linens, and put a fresh hospital gown on Charles, who compiled without protesting.

The only response came from King, back in his crate, who meowed the entire time the orderly was in the room. When the man left, Hunter told Shannon, "Looks like our snub kept him from asking questions about King." He opened the cage door. King came out and Hunter held onto his collar. "Time to try again to see if King can connect with Charles. Tell you what, I'll tell my guards to block anyone, anyone at all, trying to get in the room this time. With no interruptions, maybe we can succeed."

He turned King loose and the cat went straight to the bed, hopped up on it, and took his position next to

Charles' shoulder. This time, Charles didn't react. His body didn't relax, nor did his eyes open.

Hands in prayer mode, Shannon turned to Hunter shaking her head.

Hunter shook a finger and mouthed the words, "Give it a few minutes."

Charles twitched. His eyes narrowed and then opened wider. He turned his head in the cat's direction. When he lifted a hand, Shannon stifled a gasp. He raised up little by little until he was in a sitting position. Again, he stroked the cat's back, once, then twice, then a third time. A loud purr let Shannon and Hunter know the two had connected.

When Shannon made a move to go to Charles, Hunter grabbed her arm and eased her back into her seat. "Not yet." She frowned but complied with his order. "We need to wait until Charles starts talking, or at least saying a word or two."

The door cracked open, and Hunter glared at the deputy. He pointed at him and mouthed the word, "Out," three times. The deputy threw up his hands. Then he had a ding–a text on his cell phone said, "It's the hospital administrator out here. He wants to talk to you. Can you come out?"

Hunter ran his hand through his hair. *What can he want? He said I could bring King in here and it's working. Now he's about to spoil everything.* Hunter tiptoed out of the room, hoping the distraction wouldn't affect Charles or King. As he opened the door, he looked back, happy to see both we're occupied with each other.

Out in the hallway, Administrator Rawlings introduced himself and the men shook hands. "Sorry to interfere when you seem to be having success with your cat, but we have a problem."

Hunter raised an eyebrow. *What kind of problem can be more important than a breakthrough in Charles' case?* He waited for an explanation.

"The storm's worse. Now we have a tornado warning." He tapped his foot. "We need to move everybody to a safe place."

"Good Lord!" Hunter slapped the side of his head. "We're just making some progress. Charles is actually petting King, my cat. I'm not a doctor, but I understand humanity. If we can just get him talking, I think he'll come out of this coma, or whatever you call it." He glared at Rawlings. "Can't you do something? A storm, or tornado, isn't as bad as this."

Rawlings placed his hand on Hunter's shoulder. "Look, I know this boy's condition is crucial. That's why I came to tell you about the situation myself. We have to follow safety regulations."

Hunter took a step back and Rawlings' hand fell off of his shoulder. "This whole damn situation is critical. Which is worse, a tornado or a boy's sanity which determines the course of the rest of his life?"

"I understand. I will tell you what I can do. I'll give orders to make this floor, specifically Charles' room, the last to be evacuated." He looked at his watch. "That'll take a while and the warning expires in about an hour. That will give you a little time to work with this cat experiment."

Announcements came blasting over the loud-speakers and Rawlings said, "It's the best I can do. I have to go now. Sorry. God bless you." He turned on his heel and was gone.

Hunter's deputies had heard the conversation, so he told them he'd give them orders shortly. At any rate, they were instructed to stay with Shannon and Charles no matter where they were taken or what happened.

Next, he had to tell Shannon about the tornado. How she'd respond, he couldn't guess. He did figure she'd have mixed emotions about choosing between tending to Charles or Karla. His advice was going to be to stay with Charles. He needed her more. Hunter could help by switching Zita to care for Karla at the Tollar Plantation.

He called Shannon into the hallway to explain everything to her. She took the news well and agreed to stay at the hospital. "With Zita, I think Karla will be comfortable and the Tollar Plantation is relatively safe. It's weathered many storms," she replied.

In five minutes, that was accomplished, much to Hunter's relief. *Now we need to use the little time we have to Charles' best advantage before they move us. But how do you go about outwitting a tornado?* He made the Sign of the Cross and touched the Mojo stone but undercut those actions by letting his doubts reign. *Why am I doing those things? I don't believe in that stuff. It's crazy. I know better. I need to go back to relying on myself and my own resources.*

Still, back in the room, Hunter had to admit that the results of Charles' interchange with King were up to the fates, not him. He, and Shannon, could only stand by and hope it all worked out–and it had to do so before they were hustled out of this room. Any disruption might upset the entire process.

After silence for ten minutes, Hunter spoke softly to Shannon. "I wish King could talk. Then he could reach Charles." He smiled. "His Majesty sure finds ways to get me to do what he wants without talking. Maybe there's hope he can…"

He heard a weak voice say, "King–His Majesty," and a smile crossed Charles' face. It wasn't a big grin, just big enough to recognize. Charles looked at Shannon, blinking as if to focus. Hunter called his name. "Charles," he said in his deepest voice, "do you know Shannon?"

With a nod, Charles turned his gaze upon Hunter, who asked. "Do you know me?"

"You - Sheriff."

"Right. Can you sit up, Charles?"

Wriggling into a seated position, Charles pulled the cat close to his chest. "He's a good cat, King is."

This time, when Shannon approached her charge, Hunter didn't stop her. She circled the boy's shoulders with her arms, careful not to disturb King. When he squeezed her back, sobs shook her entire body. "Charles, oh, Charles. I'm so glad you're talking again. Thank God!"

The hospital gown slipped down revealing a large red ring around Charles' neck. Hunter cringed at the sight of the mark from a dog collar, the source of the boy's physical and psychological malady, his loss of speech. He vowed such mistreatment resulting in trauma wasn't going to happen to this boy again. Now that Charles was back to his senses, Hunter hoped he could help in the search for Frederica. If she'd do that to her own flesh and blood, she was capable of anything, even murder. If she'd already viciously killed Judas, and maybe others they didn't know about, who'd be next?

He knew better than to push too hard too soon, but by the time this ordeal of the tornado warning was over, he could pick Charles' brain. This intelligent boy very likely knew things about his mother that he hadn't told. Maybe now he had reached the point where he could. Hunter needed all the help he could get. He had to get that woman off the streets.

Chapter 25

It turned out that the tornado warning was lifted before they had to evacuate Charles' room, so he didn't have to leave. During the waiting time, Charles talked more. His first question was, "Where's Karla?" Shannon reassured him that she was safe at home, and that seemed to satisfy him. Next, he said he was hungry, but in the chaos, everything was off schedule, no supper had been served. Hunter got him crackers and a soda from the vending machines to hold him over.

Until they received a delivery by a deputy from Zita–sandwiches, chips and a tab-top can of tuna for King–Hunter and Shannon hadn't realized they were hungry, too. Zita called and apologized for only having peanut and jelly to offer, and she was thrilled to hear about the progress with Charles. "What's next?" she asked.

"I'm biding my time. He's too fragile to be rushed. I'll keep you posted."

Hunter waited until after Charles had a meal before broaching the touchy subject of the kidnapping. He approached that incident very slowly and cautiously, letting the boy respond at his own pace.

Setting it up to be pleasant, Hunter said, "I think you may be able to go home tomorrow, Charles."

Charles' eyes brightened as he edged to the side of the bed and slid down, standing beside it. "I'm okay. Can't I go now?" His bottom lip curled downward. "I want to see my sister. I need to be sure she's alright." He took a step forward and stumbled.

Hunter caught him. "You're not quite ready, Son. Let's wait until the doctor comes and see what he says."

In a loud voice, Charles insisted. "But I want to see Karla." He made two fists and clasped them next to his body. "Mama, I'm scared Mama's going to try to take her. She planned to do that at the Crossroads. She told me to bring Karla back with me. I didn't. I knew that wasn't Karla with Shannon on the ladder."

He started wheezing and Hunter lifted him back onto the hospital bed. *How did Charles know it wasn't Karla?*

His unspoken question was answered. "I saw that lady's face. When I brought the money back to Mama, I told her it wasn't Karla. I guess she got scared 'cause she didn't stop me when I left. She just ran away." His eyes clouded with tears.

Shannon sat on the other side of the bed and pulled the boy close in a tight hug. He didn't move from her arms. Hunter had to hold his breath to keep from crying out at the bittersweet scene. Empathy for all this child had been through overcame him. Charles was a brave young boy who'd weathered a storm much worse than any tornado. What could hurt more than rejection? This went beyond that; it included physical and mental torture. No wonder he shrank into a shell. How could he exist in such a world? It was a miracle he came alive again.

Hunter stood. "This is enough for tonight. I'm leaving." He turned to Shannon. "Both of you need a good night's rest. I'll see you in the morning."

#

King seemed to be as glad to be back in his own territory as Hunter was. After fresh food and water, the cat snuggled in bed with its face on Hunter's neck. The collar rubbing against his skin reminded Hunter of Charles' being restrained by one and he shivered. He dreaded what Charles might say if he was able to talk about that.

His cell phone interrupted his thoughts. It was Shannon and she had a tremor in her voice. "I'm so happy, and relieved. The doctor came after you left. He was astonished by the change in Charles. He said he can go home tomorrow." She paused. "Charles is asleep now. I'm sick of this place and I'm glad to leave, but I don't know what I'll face at home. Geez, I sure hope Charles doesn't revert. I don't think I could handle that."

"I think he'll be okay. He seems steady. The guards can escort you home and stay until I get there. I have some paperwork to do at the office. Let me know when you're settled in and I'll come over."

"Okay, take it easy with the questions. I know, you've been very cautious not to upset him. But we don't want to do anything to cause…"

"Never mind. I understand. I'm experienced at this, Shannon. It's my life's work." Times when he played Bad Cop; Good Cop came to mind. He always played the good cop. "Like most people," he continued, "I've handled personal crisis, too." A memory of when he was still a teenager flashed through his mind–a girl, his family, her family, a confrontation, a devastating climax. Then all went sour and his life changed forever. He struggled to push the disturbing thoughts out of his mind. He pleaded for something he'd neglected to plead for before. "Give me a chance and I'll work through this. It'll have a successful conclusion."

"Sorry, Hunter," Shannon backed down. "I didn't mean to underestimate you. I realize you know what you're doing. I guess it's just the attorney in me–I kind of want to be in charge." A nervous chuckle lightened the mood. "Get some rest. I'll call you when we're home."

When the unpleasant event of the past tried to invade his thoughts again, Hunter got up, went to the kitchen and made coffee. On his heels, King followed.

"You want to help? You can't." Hunter drank a cup of coffee and it took his mind off of disturbing issues, but they were replaced by Charles' kidnapping, another stressful time. He framed questions in his mind, wrote down a few, and returned to bed. King climbed onto the foot of it, curled up, and was soon snoring. Now that Hunter knew the approach he was going to take, he laid his head down to rest and fell asleep in ten minutes.

Before dawn the next morning, a loud "Meow" and a scratching on the top sheet next to Hunter's arm awakened him before the alarm sounded.

"It's not time to get up yet, King." Hunter yawned. "The clock hasn't gone off." He rolled over and the cat jumped off of the bed, adding meows in sequence. "Okay, you want food." Hunter got out of bed and walked barefoot to the kitchen. He spilled water next to the food bowl but didn't wipe it up. Then he made coffee and went to the bathroom while it perked.

Looking in the mirror, his red eyes stared back at him. *Guess this pressure is getting to me.* He yawned again. *I need more sleep, but I was gone all day yesterday. I need to get to the station and see where things stand before Shannon calls. After I interview Charles, I've got to get back to the chase and catch Frederica before she takes off again.*

Hoping Charles could give them some clues about Frederica's hideouts, Hunter shaved and took a shower, then dressed for work. On the way, he speculated about the day's events. Chances were that Shannon wouldn't call until after noon. He could get a lot done there in four hours, if nothing interrupted him. He'd brought lunch to save time.

Before he got in the door at the office, Zita intercepted him. "Just got a call from Daryl. He's chasing a speeder on Highway 61 and he says it looks like Frederica. Two people are in the car. It's a different one, a Camry."

Hunter listened to the report. Daryl was traveling at 100 miles per hour. "I'm close and my siren's on, but she's ignoring it. Send backup." Without other warning, brakes squealing could be heard, and then there was a crash.

Hunter called out, "What's happened? Are you okay, Deputy?" No response. He heard Zita contacting 911. He grabbed his holster and snapped it in place on his shoulder. Then he dashed out of the station and raced to his car.

He made it to the scene at the same time the ambulance, fire truck, and two other patrol cars arrived. The police car had crashed into a telephone pole on a curve. It burrowed into the ditch on its left side. It was crumpled back to the rear seat on the right. Daryl sat moaning in the driver's seat where the airbag had exploded. It probably saved his life. The paramedics pulled him from the car, and he was able to stand, but he was reeling. One of them steadied him.

Hunter rushed over. "Are you alright?"

Daryl blinked. "I think so." He looked at his arms and legs. "A little wobbly, though."

"Did you see where the other car went?"

He pointed ahead to a road on the right. "She turned there right after she sideswiped another car. That driver swung around and chased her. I wasn't close enough to get a license number on the car she hit, but here's a partial number on Frederica's–it's a Tennessee license - 62 are the last two numbers."

Hunter radioed orders to search for both cars. Against his protests, they took Daryl off in the ambulance. "I'll check on you later," Hunter promised. How much later, he didn't know.

Hunter joined the search himself but was too far behind to catch up. The patrol cars hadn't spotted the cars they were chasing yet. So, he returned to the station, calling about Daryl to discover he checked out of the ER in good shape.

Then he called Shannon to find they were being driven home by one of the deputies. "Give us a couple of hours to freshen up and have lunch. Then Charles will be ready to talk to you?" She said to her seatmate, "Won't you, Charles?" telling Hunter he nodded.

A minute later Hunter got a text from Shannon: "He's chewing on his thumbnail. He's never done that before. Regression due to stress? I'm worried."

Hunter texted her back and she shielded the message with her hand so Charles couldn't see it. "Ignore that action. It's temporary. It'll go away. Time heals. Later." He had to reassure her even though he wasn't convinced what he told her was true. But time did heal. He learned that from personal experience.

By noon, they had no luck with the chase, so they called it off. Nor did they have luck with the partial license number. Not enough to go on. Daryl came to the station and from his description it had been Frederica in the car. He said the passenger looked like a man, but he couldn't be sure.

"I'm sure of one thing, Frederica is not alone in this. She's getting those cars somewhere. Maybe from Memphis. Who? How the hell do I know? Sounds like a gang, doesn't it?"

Daryl shook his head. "I sure wish I could've caught her. We need to put an end to this."

Hunter stuck out his bottom lip. "We will, Daryl. We will."

A phone call from Shannon let him know they were ready to meet with him. Hunter said, "I may not be back today. Hold the fort," and he left. Far from ready for this ordeal, he summoned his sturdiness. "Give me strength for this inquisition. It's unlike anything I've ever faced." It was as close as he came to prayer. It didn't stop there. Hunter took the Mojo stone from his pocket, rubbed it once, and put it back where it came from. Despite his claims of disbelief, the odd sense of relief that overcame him couldn't be denied.

Chapter 26

Between times of gasping out the grizzly details of being on a leash, sleeping in the back of the store or in the car duct-taped, and subsisting on chips, crackers, Vienna sausage, and deviled ham, Charles chewed on his thumb or petted King whom Hunter brought along with him.

He told them even though his mama and Judas slapped him around, he didn't try to leave because she said if he did she'd get Karla. "Mama and a man I never saw talked about killing Judas," he said in a shaky voice. He knew Judas was killed, but he didn't see the killing or the body. Unlike he normally spoke, he blurted out incomplete sentences. "Judas bad. Why Mama hate me? What wrong?"

Shannon replied in the only way she could. "Your mama has a problem, Charles. Something's wrong in her head."

Hunter nodded. "She needs help, but we won't let her near you, or Karla, again. Don't worry." Using the word *crazy* would be too strong. It might set Charles off again. They had to try to keep him at ease as much as possible.

Consoling him wasn't easy. Comfort food or milk and cookies didn't do the trick. He kept asking for Karla, but neither Shannon nor Hunter thought it was a good idea for her to hear the gory situation Charles had been in. So they kept her upstairs in her bedroom with a guard.

After about an hour, Hunter got to the big question. "Do you have any idea where Frederica went, Charles?"

Charles shook his head.

"Did she talk about any place or call any names of people?"

Charles bit his thumb. "Just Judas."

"How about the man who came around? Did you ever see him?"

Picking up King, Charles scratched his ears as he looked down at them. This time he was more coherent. "No, but I was in the back room and I heard him tell her, 'Follow Harley to Memphis. Play your games. Get another car there. Don't get me involved. What happened to Judas can happen to you.'" He shrugged. "That's all I heard."

She's in with some big-time criminals. Hmm, maybe Charles heard more than he thought. I'll try again. "You were at the Crossroads, Charles. Do you think she'd go back there?"

Squinting, Charles held onto King with both hands. He held the animal to his chest. Letting out big sobs, he said. "We stayed there - couple of nights–way back in the woods in a car." Tears flooded his cheeks. "That pit bull - on a leash - she beat it to death - took leash/collar for me."

So that's what happened to the pit bull in the stolen car.

"What weapon did she use?"

"Big limb. Poor dog." He held King up and stared at him. "I hate…Mama!" He sucked in his bottom lip. "Oh, wait. She buried a plastic bag and…by a tree…a big *F* was already carved on the tree trunk. The tree may be the one you hid in."

Aha! Finally, a clue. No matter what she buried, money, or drugs, she'll go back for it. Probably at night; maybe tonight. I've got to beat her to it. Then we can watch the area and catch her.

He gave the boy a hug. "You've been a big help, Charles. Now you can be with Karla. Don't worry. Everything's under control."

Telling Shannon, "I mean it," he left with the most hope he'd had since this fiasco began. *I might just hide in that same tree again. Look out, Frederica, here I come!*

Before dark, camouflaged deputies were in strategic, but hidden, spots surrounding the area. They found the tree marked with the *F*, but to avoid alerting the culprit, they didn't dig up the bag. They could catch her off guard while she dug it up. Plus, it would be indisputable evidence of guilt, proving it belonged to her.

The deputies and the sheriff communicated with radios. Any traffic was reported immediately. No walkers passed by, but cars came and went. Three Camrys were scrutinized but none bore the last two numbers Daryl gave them. None stopped anyhow. The plan was to spend the night, if necessary. They didn't have to. At 9 p.m. a Camry pulled way off of the highway onto the grass and as close to the tree as possible, behind other trees and bushes. A woman got out and took a shovel from its trunk. Then she went to the base of the large oak and started digging.

Before she tossed the first shovel of dirt, a bevy of officers encircled her, flooding the area with flashlight beams. Her mouth dropped open. She swung the shovel at one deputy's head, but he dodged, and she missed her mark. A car coming from nowhere pulled up, forcing deputies to make a path for it or risk getting run over.

Frederica took advantage of the confusion to try to hop into the car which slowed down, but Hunter ran up and jerked her away, threw her to the ground, and snapped on handcuffs. The driver, a male, fled the scene. Hunter motioned two deputies to follow the man. He ordered a couple of other officers to, "Read this woman her rights. Book her for murder and kidnapping."

Trying to pull free, Frederica turned and yelled at Hunter. "Murder? I didn't kill anybody. You can't charge me with kidnapping. Charles is my own child, you bastard!"

"Add child abuse." Ignoring her repeated protests, Hunter rushed to his hidden car. Jumping into it, he got onto the highway and joined the chase.

He radioed to the remaining deputies to dig up the loot and let him know what it was. Before long, they reported that the bag was full of drugs, thousands of dollars worth. Hunter suspected Frederica had taken those from Judas after he was murdered. Another reason to believe she was the culprit who killed him for the drugs. He didn't think they'd find a weapon, since Charles saw her bury the bag but didn't mention seeing anything else go into that hole, but he asked anyhow. "Negative," the deputy replied.

You win some; you lose some. Right now, I'm happy to capture Frederica. Whoever that guy driving the car is–her accomplice–we'll get him too. He didn't see any of his men's cars, but he checked with them and kept driving the same route, hoping they were all on the right track and that they'd catch up with the man, hang onto his tail, and eventually stop him.

It didn't happen. Along the way, he'd taken a turn and eluded them. Maybe he went into the woods. If so, they'd have to get more dogs and try to hunt him down, but that would take until tomorrow. If he had the backup of a gang, he may have had another car stashed somewhere or someone ready to pick him up and take him far away. After three hours of circling around,

Hunter reluctantly called off the chase. "We'll start over in the morning. Ten-four."

The chase was over literally, but it still remained in Hunter's mind. At home, he didn't go to bed. He sat in his recliner with King in his lap, mulling over possibilities and planning a strategy. Switching to wallowing in the glory of capturing Frederica, he found it ludicrous that she denied the murder, especially since she had those valuable drugs. She also had the nerve to claim Charles as her son when she'd treated the boy like her worst enemy and denied her actions were a kidnapping. "That galls me! I'll fix her in court. She'll never get out of jail." He banged the table next to his chair and King jumped to freedom.

After sleeping in his chair all night, Hunter awakened with tense muscles. He walked around the room to loosen up. Coffee and a piece of toast helped. It took less time than a full meal. He had a new plan, one he wanted to implement right away. A quick shower refreshed him, and he was ready for a new day.

Radio reports didn't reveal anything new, but he checked in. "I'm on my way to Dewayne's barn. Double-checking his whereabouts last night. I'll recheck everything at the Get – 'n - Go store, too, to be sure we didn't miss anything. Over and out."

First, he went to the barn. Looking around let him know Dewayne was no longer sleeping there. His radio was gone. So was the machete with the handle broken off. *Why didn't I take it before? Damn! Sure as shooting, it was the murder weapon, but how? Hmm, it wouldn't be hard to break off the handle after killing somebody with it. And I fell for that innocent ploy. What a fool I was. With all my experience, I should know better.* He didn't leave empty-handed. On his way out, he picked up a Band-Aid with blood on it.

His next stop was the store. It was still closed and surrounded with police tape. Hunter ducked under the police tape and used a key he'd brought along to open the door wearing plastic gloves. Then, in his mind's eye, he tried to recreate the scene. Visualizing a few whacks including dismembering Judas' head and arm, he next approached the cash register and opened it. Earlier, evidence showed the murderer had taken all the cash that was in it. He tried to lift the tray, but it wouldn't come all the way out, so he pulled on it until it broke free.

Underneath was a newsclip about an event honoring a man named Wayne Kingston for hiring young trustees from the local jail to work in his restaurant in Jackson. It detailed how Kingston implemented this program. The prisoners were delivered to work daily in a prison van and picked up at closing time. The article claimed that Kingston's compassion had resulted in many prisoners turning their lives around. Because he'd just had to admit being remiss in collecting evidence himself, he didn't fault the investigators for this mistake of missing it.

The dinner was set at the Holiday Inn in Jackson on this same day at 6 p.m. Hunter's brain whirled. *Could Wayne Kingston be Dewayne? A first-class hypocrite? Was he really a King, the head of the Kingsmen Gang? A man with two names and two faces. Was he faking being a drunk? Not impossible.*

His cell phone rang. "Sheriff, this is Dewayne. I got a job in Jackson as a busboy in a fancy restaurant, so I had to leave. Just wanted to warn you not to pay any attention to what that woman you arrested tells you. I didn't have nothin' to do with her. If she tries to pin Judas' murder on me, don't listen to her. She did it. She'll say anything to get off the hook. You know she's a liar and she's crazy. Phone's dyin'." It clicked off.

Coincidence of coincidences. Or can that guy read my mind? How'd he know about Frederica getting arrested? But news travels fast. Funny, he did call me early on about her being in this store, but that could've been a set-up to throw me off guard regarding his game. Daryl suspects him and he has good instincts. The machete's gone. Do I have enough evidence to pop his balloon at that party tonight? He put the paper in an envelope and took it to the car. *I need time to sort this out.*

Hunter had a hunch. He returned to the hole where they'd dug up the drugs. Maybe Frederica had been there before. He got a shovel from his trunk and dug a couple of feet deeper. Sure enough, he saw the edge of a blade and after tossing out more dirt, he found a piece of wood. Pulling them out, he retrieved a machete and its matching handle. *Bingo! I bet testing will reveal blood on this blade, maybe on the handle, too."*

Two hours later, the lab proved him right. Using the Band-Aid, they were able to match the blood to Dewayne's. Frederica's might show up, too, so could fingerprints. He'd also looked up Wayne Kingston but found no concrete link to an alternate identity.

The clock struck noon as they left Cleveland. The drive to Jackson would only take two hours. They'd have time to find the location of the venue, ironically Central Church Auditorium, and park. With GPS that shouldn't be a problem. Six o'clock couldn't come soon enough. He called in Zita and Daryl. "We're going to Jackson. I've made arrangements with them to make the arrest. To justify it, I fudged a little by saying we lost him in pursuit in a car chase; I just didn't say when it happened. Anyhow, they know exactly what's going on. They sent the dogs. If I could, I'd bring those dogs back with me; we won't need them." He explained the entire situation to them, and excitement filled the air.

The trip was easy and quick. Traffic was light and they only made one rest stop. GPS directed them to the church. Inside, a ticket-taker asked for their invitations. Hunter opened his jacket and exposed his badge. "Don't need one. We're here on police business." Before she could protest, he walked past her to the church auditorium.

The speaker was beaming. "Mr. Kingston has been a friend ever since he opened his restaurant in our city," he said. "He saved some of our young people by hiring them and monitoring them to lead them in a different direction with his innovative program."

He turned to the man now standing next to him in a five-hundred-dollar suit. Holding a plaque high, he said, "Now we'd like to present you…"

Mouth agape, the speaker followed Hunter, Zita, and Daryl with his eyes as they reached the speaker's table and all three walked around behind it amidst stares and gasps from the audience.

"Mr. Kingston," Hunter announced, "you are under arrest for the murder of Judas Martin." He read him his rights.

While Zita cuffed the honoree, Daryl took his arm and led him away from the table.

"Call my attorney," the prisoner told the female taking notes. Then he spoke to the audience. "This is all a huge mistake, folks," he assured people now clamoring to help him but being pushed aside by the three deputies. At the door he called out, "I'll be released in an hour. Keep that plaque. We'll soon reschedule this event."

Hunter waited until they put Kingston in the back seat of the car with Daryl and pulled out onto the highway before he announced they were taking him to Cleveland.

"What the Hell? No, I'm not!" He screamed the protest while trying to wriggle free. It did no good,

Hunter gave him time to calm down and then he lit into Kingston with accusations.

"Did you really think I was some hick cop you could fool with your drunken, homeless act, DEWayne?" He embellished his statement saying, "I had you pegged shortly after the first act you tried." He glanced in the rear view mirror. "But you do look different in that fancy suit."

"What are you talking about, Sheriff? I'm no drunk, and we've never met. I haven't ever been to Bolivar County, much less Cleveland."

"The hell you haven't. I have evidence…"

Kingston leaned forward, pressing his arms against the back of the driver's seat. "Wait a minute. This must be my twin brother you're talking about. I'm Wayne and he's DEWayne. Is he in trouble again? Damn! Now he's dragging me down with him. I managed to keep him a secret. Then he keeps popping up. Oh, God, he's had minor scrapes before–but murder? I can't bail him out of this one." He hung his head.

Hunter bit the corner of his lip. *Could this be true? Or is it just a slick trick, an excuse he's making up to get out of trouble? Either way, this guy is going to jail until he can prove his claim. It shouldn't be hard to check and verify, either.* He bit down harder and drew blood. Wiping it off with a tissue, he had second thoughts. *On the other hand, maybe I'm not giving Wayne enough credit. Hell, with his money, respected position, and clout, he may have proof all set up.*

Melody of Malice

Chapter 27

All the way to Cleveland Wayne pleaded his case. "Once you hear my story, Sheriff, I think you'll take me back to Jackson and let me go, or at least release me without bail. You see," he said, "I'm a victim of circumstances. Dewayne and I are identical twins, in appearance, but it ends there. Our lifestyles are exact opposites."

To explain, he started with his early life. "It took a lot of time, money, and arm-twisting, but I found out my history. I grew up in an orphanage in Pascagoula, Mississippi. I wasn't lucky enough to be adopted, not until I reached age twelve. An older couple took pity on me and raised me as their foster child. They were borderline poor, but fine, upstanding citizens, and I knew they loved me. They're both dead now, but they encouraged me to go to college and that was the best advice I ever had. They also taught me to be generous– you saw evidence of that with the event in my honor." He paused but his bragging statement received no acknowledgment.

"No need to go into detail about my success, so I'll move on to Dewayne's upbringing. You see, I never knew I had a twin until one day I was walking down the street on a business trip to Biloxi and across the street I spotted a man who looked exactly like me, even with his scruffy beard. I did a double-take. The saying that everyone has a twin somewhere came to mind, but seeing an exact replica of yourself is a real shock. I had to know more, so I ran after him and caught up."

He cleared his throat and continued after a short hesitation. "It was the worst thing I ever did, the biggest mistake I ever made. His childhood and teenage years contradicted mine. Maybe nurture does take preference over nature. Dewayne was shifted from one foster home to another. No stability. The last one turned him over to cousins in the underworld when he was twelve. They taught him to be a bum. He ran away and became homeless. Everyone lost track of him. By the time he was eighteen his mold was set."

He sucked in his breath. "When he found out about me, he used me every chance he got. Oh, I wasn't a complete sucker. By then, I was a well-respected citizen of Jackson. I used my resources, and I had some clout. So, I investigated Dewayne. It wasn't easy to do, but I achieved it. Most of what he told me about his past was true. Still, I had my pride, so I didn't let anyone know I had a twin. Keeping him a secret cost me, too, but I felt it was worth it. Finally, I got tired of it but when I threatened to cut him off, he countered with, 'I'll tell the world about you and me; how's that hit ya?' Oh, by the way, I'm sure you can hear the differences in the way we speak."

That got Hunter's attention. *He's right. Dewayne isn't articulate at all. But can I swallow this line? He could fake it. Just how many details can he come up with on the spur of the moment?*

His thoughts were interrupted by Wayne's next words. "My name was Kingston, so Dewayne changed his to Roi, meaning King. He's slick. That got him in with the Kingsmen gang in Jackson where he hoped to fulfill his goal of becoming a big shot in the criminal world." He chuckled. "But he never quite made it. Didn't have the guts to…Wait a minute! Maybe he did."

"Are you thinking Dewayne did commit murder?" Hunter pulled into a rest stop and parked. Then he turned to face Wayne in the back seat. Daryl and Zita also stared at their prisoner. "Has he ever mentioned the name Judas Martin to you?"

Wayne shook his head. "No, the first time I heard that name was when you said it. He leaned his head into the palms of his handcuffed hands. In a muffled voice he said, "He's still my twin brother. I can't believe he's capable of that."

A logical thought took over Hunter's mind: *Would it be smart for Wayne to set up a brother that didn't exist and expose himself to being accused of murder, if the truth were that he, Wayne, and Dewayne, are one and the same person?*

He needed a break to sort those thoughts and maybe come to the truth. *Whatever the truth is.* All four occupants of the car got out and went to the restroom. Zita and Daryl walked arm in arm with Dewayne, covering his hands with his coat to avoid frightening other people in the area. On the way out, Hunter bought snacks from the vending machines for everybody, and they took them to the car to eat.

Still cuffed, Wayne managed to handle his food after Daryl unwrapped the cheese crackers and took the screw top off of the Coke. "Have I convinced you that my brother, not me, is the person you should be after?"

"Why should I believe you, Mr. Kingston? No, it will take a lot of evidence to convince me. You're still going to my jail in Cleveland."

He clenched his teeth. "I have my rights. When can I make my phone call? I need to check with my lawyer. He's probably on his way to meet me, and he's good, very good."

If that was a warning or a threat, it failed to impress Hunter. In Dallas, he'd been up against the best attorneys in the world. He could handle this one from Jackson. To Wayne, he replied, "You'll get your phone call when we get to the station."

Wayne raised his voice. "Why can't I make my call on your cell phone?"

"Because I say so." Hunter started the car. "Right now, I'm busy driving."

Muttering an obscenity, Wayne dropped the cracker wrapper full of crumbs and the half-full Coke bottle on the floorboard. The soda spilled and he said with a sarcastic sneer, "Sorry about that." Then he leaned back in the seat and pretended to be snoring.

"I'd rather hear that than his made-up excuses," Daryl said, evoking a snigger from Hunter. *Daryl expressed his opinion of Wayne's diatribe, but I won't determine mine until I've seen all the proof Wayne claims to have. I'll sure keep in mind how surreptitious criminals can be. To be honest and fair, though, I'll also remember that truth can be stranger than fiction.*

#

Wayne Kingston's lawyer arrived early the next morning. Dressed in a suit as expensive as his clients, Mr. Maurice Wood, stood six-foot tall and weighed over two hundred pounds. He introduced himself saying, "My name is Wood, and I *wood* help anyone I could." He followed with a hearty laugh.

Hunter had heard of this attorney who broke the rules in court and used ruthless methods to win his cases. He worked for the Kingsmen gang and had gotten many criminals off without serving a day in jail. Hunter's suspicions took on strength. This kind of lawyer usually served the guilty. More intent than ever, Hunter spent the day researching the list of names and places Wayne had given him.

The orphanage had closed, so he dug into records, but Wayne told him they called him Wayne Smith until the Kingstons changed his name to theirs. He put a deputy on it to dig deeper and discovered the facility used Smith for many orphans' last names. It was easy to remember. He checked on the deceased foster parents. They did exist and they had a foster child listed in a census. He got neighbors' phone numbers but in twenty plus years many had moved, two had gone to nursing homes, and a couple died. A dead end.

Hunter decided to throw presenting proof into Wayne's lap. He told Wood and the lawyer screamed out his reply, "You're the sheriff; you know the burden of proof is up to you! A client is innocent until proven guilty."

Walking away, Hunter said, "But you have to prove your client has an identical twin. Otherwise, it's his blood on that machete and his DNA will show up, too." He didn't say so then, but he had another ace in the hole: He'd move Frederica to the cell next to Wayne's in the middle of the night with a hidden tape recorder.

She'd spent her days there claiming she didn't kill Judas. If that were true, or if both were guilty as charged, she wouldn't take the punishment alone. Criminals were notorious for giving each other up to save their own skins. Frederica was afraid of that gang getting revenge, but if she became angry enough, in a crazy rage, she might lose her cool and rat on Wayne. He had to act fast. Frederica would be transported to the Bolivar County Correction Center tomorrow and Wayne was scheduled to go before the judge in the morning. How it would play out, Hunter didn't know, but he assigned Zita and Daryl to work the midnight shift and to move Frederica. Their actions would cause less suspicion than his. "I don't know what will happen, but I hope to find out tonight."

But that didn't happen. They walked Frederica in front of Wayne's cell, making sure she had time to recognize him. She rattled the bars yelling at him and calling him a murderer. But the wall between the two prisoners prevented a physical confrontation and Wayne spun his tale to her. She calmed down and quit ranting.

The next morning when Hunter listened to the tape, he was astounded. "That's out of character for that woman to believe anybody, much less Kingston. Why didn't she fall for our trick?"

Neither Daryl nor Zita had a good answer. "She's unpredictable, Zita replied.

"She's a nutcase, but maybe she's smarter than we think and knows when to shut up."

Later that day, both Wayne and Frederica were hauled off to the Bolivar County Correction Center for further processing. Temporarily, the case was out of Hunter's hands.

At the end of his shift, Hunter went home. When he opened his door, before he could catch King, the cat slipped past him. "Go ahead," Hunter yelled at his back, "but don't expect your supper until I eat mine." He went into his bedroom and dropped his jacket on the bed. Then he stepped into something and looked down. The suitcase laid open and shredded paper covered the floor in front of it. "Damn you King. How in the hell did you get that case open? I guess I left it unlocked. You made another mess. I'm going to kill you!"

Stooping down, he collected the paper into a pile. Then his hand struck something. Right in the middle, he found a record. His heart pounded. No label. He turned it over. Nothing on the other side, either. How it got there, he couldn't figure out. *I guess I just fumbled around and missed it. The paper was stuck together. Man, I've got to get to a record player and find out what's here. Hell, it could be blank.*

On the way, he saw V and called to him. "King got out again. Please put him back inside when you see him."

V waved and nodded. "Will do."

They had a record player at the station, so Hunter went back there. "Found something," he told Zita who followed him into a room. He put the record on, and it blasted out the lyrics to *Bad News Blues* in Goldie's voice.

"Bingo! What a find," Hunter said as he watched a huge grin cross Zita's face. "Won't Shannon be surprised."

"She sure will. You know what, Hunter, that tune sounds a lot like the one she came up with. I've heard her sing it."

Putting the record back in its sleeve, Hunter said, "I'm taking this home and hiding it. I don't trust leaving it here. I'll call Shannon and let her know the good news. Seems like she'd be the legal owner, but we need advice to be sure."

On the way home with his newfound treasure, he speculated how many people might lay claim to this valuable find. But he was too tired to guess. He'd find out soon enough anyhow.

Chapter 28

Shannon was elated. When Hunter took it to her house, he listened to the record played on the old record player beaming. "Now I can sing it, make it my song, in Goldie's honor and with the tune he intended. I may just pursue a new career as a singer. I need a change. So do the kids. I'll get them tutors and they can go on tour with me." She looked around. "I'll keep the Tollar Plantation, but right now we need to get away from all this chaos."

Hunter agreed. She'd have to return for the trial, but for now, a change of venue would be beneficial. He told her, "There's a lot to be settled about ownership, Shannon, but I don't see any reason you can't get a copy of the record."

She frowned. "This original should be mine, and mine alone. I need it, Hunter. I still want to open that museum. I could get enough money from that record to do it. Plus, I have engagements to sing; that'll help, too."

He understood her concern, so he said, "I'll do whatever I can to help."

#

Nothing much happened in the next couple of weeks, then they set an early date for the trials of Frederica and Wayne. They'd be separate, but in consecutive weeks. When one was over, the other would start. Wayne would be charged with first degree murder. Frederica was charged as an accessory to murder, kidnapping, and child abuse.

In Wayne's trial, Attorney Maurice Wood put on a fantastic act, but it didn't work. No concrete proof of a twin brother for Wayne was presented. The prosecutor researched well. He located old orphanage records with a last name assigned to Dewayne–Jones–but two homes they said the boy was sent to were occupied by new tenants and the third was torn down, now a vacant lot.

Wayne's attorney produced papers like a birth certificate and school report cards; all turned out to be fake. Places of employment records didn't match with those employers' records. Maurice claimed they just didn't keep good records, but that fell on deaf ears.

The blood and the DNA both proved to be Wayne's. With no twin to get him off of the hook, the game was up. In addition, Frederica came forth with an accusation, "Wayne killed Judas Martin; I saw him do it."

Unfortunately for Frederica, the next week, Wayne testified against her. It didn't help his cause, but he got even. She had lesser charges but was convicted of all three. Her sentence added up to a life sentence. The attorney's request for insanity went nowhere. She'd spend the rest of her days in prison.

In Wayne's case the Band-Aid did the trick. When the prosecutor asked Hunter about it, he suggested they check Wayne's wrist for a scar. They did and finding one on his hand proved he was Dewayne. The jury saw right through his story and he was convicted of murder in the first degree.

Losing his first case in fifteen years took Mr. Wood down a peg or two. He raved that he'd appeal to the highest court, if necessary, claiming everything in the case was unfair and that he'd win in a retrial. Despite protests from supporters that Wayne Kingston, a well-respected citizen, was falsely convicted, he remained in jail.

Hunter was gleeful. All of his hard work investigating paid off. The murder was solved. He planned a party partly to celebrate both the results of the case and Shannon's success with singing and finding another record of Goldie's. She could sell it and that would enable her to finish the museum. How she'd juggle running it and have singing gigs, he didn't know. But it wasn't his problem. She'd have to figure that out herself.

It had been a while since the barbeque he'd hosted for his staff, but he thought the successful convictions and Shannon's good fortune called for one. He loved to cook and was an expert, especially with his top-of-the-line Erik appliances. Using them simplified the chore.

This time, he planned a cornish hen dinner with fresh green beans, wild rice and gravy, and his special garlic bread with melted butter, lemon juice, cheddar cheese, and oregano. It always made a hit. He'd start with Caesar salad and finish with pound cake topped with lemon glaze and vanilla ice cream.

First, he checked his sterling silver, thinking about the story about it that his mother enjoyed telling. When his mom and dad first married, someone broke into their apartment and took a silver chest. But it was filled with cheap flatware. So his mother used what was left every day from then on–her good silver. Hunter developed the same habit.

Next, Hunter checked his bar. To suit everybody's tastes, he'd need more variety of liquor. He made a trip to the liquor store nearby and picked up wine and other spirits. At the grocery store, checking his list, he made sure to have all the food supplies he needed too. Set for Saturday evening, he looked forward in anticipation. Getting there was half the fun. Time to relax. It was going to be a great party.

Only adults attended, Zita, Daryl, Chan, Shannon, V, and Levenia. After cocktails, when dinner was served, they agreed not to discuss the case. "Let's just keep it upbeat," Hunter suggested. As they enjoyed the gourmet fare, Shannon leaned over and kissed him on the cheek. She bragged about his expertise in the culinary field, and Zita flinched. But it led all of the others to chime in with their own compliments.

As people planned to depart, King darted out of the open door and escaped. Way ahead of his pursuers, he was soon out of sight. Shannon and Zita were first to go look for him. In five minutes, Shannon called out from some bushes, "I've found him!"

At this opportunity alone with Hunter, Shannon moved closer to him. "This was such a great night. I have one concern about leaving. I don't want to be away from you, Hunter. You've done so much for me."

Zita picked up King and from the corner of her eye she saw Shannon kiss Hunter who backed off right away. "Now wait, Shannon, there's nothing between us. We've never even had a date. We're just friends," he told her bluntly.

Zita came from the shadows, cuddling King. "Am I interrupting something?"

Hunter moved to her side. "No, not at all." He took King and swatted him. "You bad cat. I give you a good home and what do you do? You run off every chance you get."

He turned around to face the two women. "I've got to get this boy upstairs, or he'll try to get away again." He laughed. "And I don't want to chase him till daybreak. Good night, Ladies."

Zita took his dismissal as amusing, but Shannon stomped off and headed to her car grumbling, "Now how do you like that? Hunter has never acted this way before."

Taking note of Shannon's flirtatious efforts set Zita thinking. She and Hunter hadn't dated either, not exactly. But they'd eaten many meals together, studied cases late at night, and shared ideas. They could almost read each other's minds. That involved a special kind of interaction. It led to a relationship with true communication–a unity almost indescribable. It appeared that Hunter had not realized how close they really were. It was time for her to take over and make a move.

At seven the next morning, Zita knocked on Hunter's door. He answered wearing a robe and slippers. Tying the robe's sash, he asked, "What's wrong? Why are you here so early?"

"Nothing's wrong. I'm about to set something straight, Hunter." She reached up, pulled his face close to hers, and gave him a big kiss.

He kissed her back. For a minute, he didn't back away. Then he held her at arm's length. She looked straight into his eyes. "I've waited long enough for you to make a move. Now it's my turn. Hunter, I love you. Will you marry me?"

Even though his mouth fell wide open, Hunter couldn't speak. Finally, he managed a statement. "You don't know what you're asking, Zita." He sank onto the sofa and she sat beside him. The corners of his mouth dropped. "I'm a married man. I never told you. I never tell anyone."

He put his arm around her shoulders. "It was a long time ago. It's been over forever, but I never got a divorce. I didn't want to remarry. My job became my love, my life." Tears oozing from Zita's eyes caused him to pause, then he gave her a squeeze. "Please don't cry. Look, I sense a special feeling between us. Something almost spiritual, and you know I'm not spiritual. I've fought the temptation to ask you out, and more, but I took my marriage vows seriously. Time passing notwithstanding."

He took her hand in his. "Let me tell you the whole story. I was nineteen years-old and bagging groceries. Kourtney was seventeen and still in high school. She worked in Customer Service in the same store. We fell in love, or thought we did, on our first date–love at first sight. We were told that we were too young to marry, but our parents had other objections. Her family was strictly Catholic, Irish Catholics named O'Hara, and mine was die-hard Baptist."

He paused again. Clearing his throat, he continued. "Being Baptist didn't rub off on me. Anyway, I can equate to Goldie and Eleanor because Kourtney and I did what they did, we ran off and got a Justice of the Peace to marry us, six weeks after we met."

"How long ago was this?"

"Twenty years ago." He looked at Zita. "You know what, I think the marriage may have lasted, but between her parents constantly hounding us and mine working with the same fervor to break us up, we just couldn't handle it. We gave in and split up."

Zita stared at him. "What happened to Kourtney?"

"I don't know." He sighed. "I tried to get in touch with her, but I couldn't get past her parents. I do know this: Since we didn't get a divorce, she wouldn't go against her religion and remarry."

Zita frowned. "You do know she could've gotten an annulment in the Catholic Church. That's as if the marriage never took place."

Hunter shook his head. "Wouldn't they have had to contact me? Hmm, I was still living at home. My parents may have intercepted the phone calls or mail. They could've thwarted any efforts to contact me."

"Yes, and there are ways to get around that–it's difficult, but not impossible." She looked at him and her mood changed. "Alright, Hunter, if you're interested in my proposal, why don't you try again to find out what the score really is?" She gave him a peck on the cheek. "You may not have a barrier to remarriage at all. Kourtney was very young, she could have found another man, a Catholic, and married him in the church. This could all have been settled years ago while you were too busy playing cop to think about it." She stood to leave. "I'll see you at the station."

#

Rather than return home, Zita went to the station at 7:30. Before entering, she made sure her eyes were clear. She didn't want anyone asking questions. At her desk, she stared at her computer, but her thoughts were in the clouds trying to analyze this new side of Hunter. Questions flooded her brain. *Is he still in love with*

Kourtney? Why else would he stay celibate all these years? I bet he's always had good investigative instincts, why didn't he investigate until he found out what happened to her? MEN! And people talk about women acting erratic. She entered the name *Kourtney O'Hara* in the computer. When it asked for a city and state, she made a guess, Dallas, Texas. In a few seconds, an obituary appeared. She was shocked to see the date. It was the same year Hunter said they were married.

Hunter walked into her office and sat opposite her. He couldn't see the computer screen. He spoke in a low voice. "I couldn't tell you all of the truth, Zita, but after my marriage failed, I was a wreck. I had to see a psychiatrist. I did try to contact the O'Hara's but when they cut me off, I had to drop the matter. I couldn't bear it. I vowed to stay single and put all of my energy into my job. I'm sure I could have found out what happened to Kourtney if I'd tried hard enough, but I simply didn't have the will." He sighed. "I moved away soon after it happened and never looked back. As time passed, it became a blur." He looked at her with soulful eyes.

She swung the computer screen around to face him. He read the obituary and gasped. "She's gone! That's only a couple of weeks after we broke up. She's been gone." He curled his lip. "What could have happened? She was a very healthy girl."

It was a rhetorical question. Zita made no effort to answer. She kept silent about the possibility that crossed her mind.

Hunter focused on the screen until he'd read the entire obituary. Then he rose from his chair. "This brings everything to the surface. I'm going to unravel the mystery now. There's no putting it aside this long after the fact." His blank stare told Zita he was almost in a trance, one that didn't include her. He walked out of the room in that daze.

Zita stayed put. No need for her to duplicate Hunter's efforts. The past had risen up to taunt him. The package he'd let lay dormant for twenty years was about to come unwrapped. It wouldn't take long.

It didn't. In twenty minutes, Hunter returned with several printouts in his hand. He looked hung over. His hair was askew from running his hands through it. His eyes had reddened, and his hands were shaking. Still holding the papers, he plopped into the same chair he'd vacated earlier.

Clasping his hands till his knuckles whitened, he glared at the papers. "I can't believe this, and I could shoot myself for not preventing it." Both eyebrows lifted. "Two weeks to the day after we broke up, Kourtney committed suicide with pills." His voice shook. "If I'd gone back to her, that wouldn't have happened. It's my fault."

Zita disagreed. "No, Hunter, it's not."

"Don't tell me that!" he sneered. "I should have…"

Without flinching, Zita countered, "Whatever you had done, it was going to play out the way it did. Besides, you were both kids; do you really think you knew what you were doing?" She wanted to add that it was puppy love, but that would take it too far.

Hunter got up, staggered out of her office, and straight out of the front door. Zita didn't follow. She'd let him cool off and settle down. Later, she could pursue the matter. She sighed. Any impediments to their marriage had disappeared. Still, she didn't know how Hunter would respond to her proposal. *Hell, after all these years he may refuse me anyway. Is he capable of loving me? Could be he's a confirmed bachelor.* Her hope waned.

Chapter 29

Hunter stayed home the rest of that day. He had no inclination to explain his absence or his past life to anyone. He knew Zita. She'd never tell. She'd even make an excuse for him.

Zita. Dear God, what is going to happen with her and me? After the terrible news about Kourtney, I don't know how I feel. I can't believe Zita proposed to me. That was completely unexpected.

Erratic thoughts unnerved him. He didn't know if he could allow himself to love again. Guilt about Kourtney's death made him not even want to chance a recurrence. Zita was Catholic. Would her parents object to their marriage? He realized he was considering accepting Zita and wondered if that was a sign that he loved her. He'd never felt so confused in his life.

His doorbell rang. Through the peephole, he saw it was Shannon. He cracked the door, and she batted her eyes at him. "Hi, Hunter. I think I left my scarf here last night. I was passing by and V said you were home, so I thought I'd check."

Hunter was in no mood to deal with Shannon, so he said, "Wait here, I'll look."

Before he could protest, she brushed by him and glanced around. Then she went into his bedroom.

"It wouldn't be in there," he said.

"It might," she countered. "You put our purses on your bed." She sat down on the edge of his bed. "Oh, it's comfy. Nice."

Tired of her shenanigans, he became blunt again. Motioning to her, he said, "I'm busy, Shannon. Go on home. If I find your scarf, I'll let you know. I'll send it to you."

Glaring at him, she got off of the bed. "Forget it. I wouldn't want to put you to any trouble, Sher–iff!"

He didn't care if he'd made her angry. She'd thrown herself at him one time too many. Maybe she'd stop now. Then his mind flashed back to Zita. She didn't flirt. She just came right out and asked him to marry her. Her directness struck a chord, but he wasn't sure which one.

After wandering around in a daze all day long and skipping lunch, Hunter pulled leftovers from the refrigerator at supper time. He sat down to eat, and his cell phone rang.

"Hi, Hunter," Zita said. "Look, just take your time before answering my, er, question. I know you've had a huge shock. Just keep in mind that happened long ago, okay?"

His thanks were sincere. He was relieved that Zita's statement indicated that she didn't feel rejected.

"Are you coming in tomorrow?" she asked. "Nothing much is going on. Just routine stuff. We can manage if you aren't up to it. Oh, I told them you had the flu."

"I appreciate you covering for me. I'll be okay by tomorrow." He hung up, fearing he'd break down if he continued talking. *What's wrong with me? I'm never this indecisive. Why can't I see what I'm being offered–a smart, wonderful gal for a wife, a new life. I must be crazy.* Without taking a bite, he dumped the food into the garbage disposal and went to bed. *Maybe I can make some sense of my feelings tomorrow.*

He went to sleep but not for long. A dream about a box awakened him. It took him a minute to become alert enough to realize Kourtney had mailed the engagement ring he'd given her back to him after she left. The little pearl ring was all he could afford and, after work at the grocery store, he'd cut grass for neighbors to get enough money to buy it. He was devastated that she didn't keep it as a memento of their time together. So, when he unwrapped the package and saw the jewelry box, he never opened it. He couldn't bring himself to throw it away, so he kept it with him. wherever he moved.

In the middle of the night, he awakened and thought about how this was the second box in his life recently. Feeling compelled to deal with it, he went to his closet and reached for a candy box on the shelf. He placed it in his lap, knowing the pearl ring would be there, inside in its own ring box. He sat back on the edge of the bed with butterflies in his stomach. *Do I really want to open this now?* He looked at King who'd jumped up beside him. *What purpose can it serve to unearth old memories?*

King meowed twice. "Okay, I guess that's a yes." He popped open the top of the box to expose the ring encased in velvet. "I worked hard to afford this." He pulled it loose from its slot and the velvet came out, too, revealing a paper folded several times to fit into the bottom. Taking it out, he unfolded it. In Kourtney's handwriting, a note said:

Hunter, my one and only love,

After I'm gone, I want you to know the real reason I left. I found out I was pregnant. You and I were barely getting by, so I knew we'd need help. My parents wouldn't help if we stayed married, so I went home.

Oh, Hunter, I lost the baby! I can't stand it. I gave you up for that and ——-

I can't write anymore. This is too much to bear. I'm going to end it all.

Please keep the ring to remember me by.

I'll always be your wife.

LOVE,

Kourtney

Picking up King, Hunter held him close. "I need somebody to lean on, King. Stay with me through this," he sobbed. The note was dated the day before she died. Hunter chided himself again. *If I'd read it, I may have been able to stop her. I'm as guilty of her death as she was. I loved her.* He tried to slip the ring on his pinky finger, but it wouldn't fit; it came nowhere close. Kourtney, as a teenager the first time he saw her, appeared in his mind. He wished he had some photos, but he didn't. She'd kept the two the JP took at their wedding. *I could have had a son, or a daughter, who'd be almost twenty years-old now. That didn't happen. Lots of things didn't happen.* Then he thought about the last line of the letter: *I'll always be your wife.* Without knowing it, he'd made that wish come true. At least until now.

Holding the cat's face close to his, he asked, "Am I still bound by my marriage vows, or not, King?" With one meow, King sparked a thought that made Hunter smile. The marriage vows concluded with, *Till death do us part.* Hunter stopped crying. Although many couples ignored that part of the bargain nowadays, he'd done his best to honor all of his marriage vows. Now, he'd discovered death had parted them, and it had done so almost two decades ago.

"I'm free," he told King, "If I marry Zita, I won't be breaking any vows." King meowed twice and Hunter spoke again. "That doesn't mean I'm going to do it. It only means I know now it's alright if I do. I'm still thinking." That time he didn't get a meow of approval.

Chapter 30

As Hunter stared at the pearl ring transfixed, another stone flickered in his imagination–the Mojo stone. Thinking of first one and then the other, the past resurfaced and Hunter went into a type of trance.

Why hadn't Kourtney's parents let him know about the baby? It was his child. Then he remembered that he'd left town right after she returned the ring. He'd roamed around Texas taking whatever odd jobs he could to survive, living in shabby motels much worse than the Shackem Up Inn and subsisting on fast food. He'd even cut off communication with his parents.

He had to admit that his grievance about not being notified wasn't justified. *Maybe all that happened was supposed to be to give me time to get over the breakup. Now I know about the suicide, too. But twenty years is a long time to take to adjust.*

Rubbing the smooth top of the pearl caused a memory to float to the top of his senses, the Mojo stone. No matter how hard he tried to push it out of his mind, he couldn't. He pictured Shannon picking it up the day she'd come to him asking for protection against Frederica. Her gesture had surprised him. Since she'd claimed not to believe in the Mojo, he was taken a little aback that she still had the stone. *It seems like the Mojo worked for Shannon, at least up to a point. Neither she nor the kids were killed. Although all will suffer as a result of her terrorizing them, we have Frederica in custody. She'll serve that life sentence. Her melody of malice is over. I wouldn't be surprised if that made Shannon a believer in the Mojo. It even gets me to thinking. I bet she'll always keep that stone.*

As the present came back into focus, Hunter returned the ring to its box, slipped it into the candy box, and put it back on the closet shelf. He turned to King and shook his finger. "You know what, King, as much as I'd like to avoid Shannon's advances, I'm going to pay her a visit. We've solved the rest of the problems, but we still haven't found Goldie's urn with his remains. The museum will be opening soon, and the urn needs to be in place on the grounds before then.

"It may sound crazy, but I'm beginning to put some faith into the Mojo. If that's the key to unraveling its hiding place–and if it still exists. At any rate if I have to resort to voodoo, magic, or whatever it's called, I'll do it." The clock said 3 a.m. He returned to bed and went straight to sleep.

At eight a.m. Hunter knocked on Shannon's door. She opened it with her hand on the handles of a rolling piece of luggage. "Oh, I'm surprised to see you, Hunter.

Sorry, but I'm just getting ready to leave for Biloxi." Her eyes glistened. "I'm making my first appearance there tonight. I'll be singing those songs of Goldie's we found." She patted the space over her heart. "It's going to be live on the radio. I'm so excited."

He pointed to her luggage and to a guitar case next to it. "The kids aren't going?"

"No, they have school. Levenia helped me get a sitter. It's just for a couple of days."

She headed for her car. Hunter carried the guitar while she rolled the luggage. "Would you do me a favor and check on the progress of the museum? They're finishing up the last room." She cocked her head. "Daryl and I have become *close*. He said he'd keep an eye out, too, but I always try to get a backup." Putting her bag into the trunk next to where Hunter placed the guitar, she cocked her head. "Oh, do you have some news, or did you want to ask me something?" She placed her hand on his arm and he moved it.

"I do have a question. It's, er, about the Mojo stone. Do you still have it?"

She pulled a bag from her pocket, removed the stone, and held it up. "Yep. Here it is."

Without a word, Hunter touched the top of the stone.

Shannon looked at him. "You know, it's not like me to change my mind, but *something* got me and the kids through all that chaos. We'll all suffer trauma from it for quite a while, I suspect, but we're alive." She shrugged. "Was it the Mojo? Hells bells! I don't know. I don't know if I even believe in it. I do believe in God, and that He can be anywhere, take any form He chooses, and do anything He wants. Mojo fans refer to the Father, the Son, and the Holy Spirit. Who's to say there *can't* be a connection? Catholics have their medals and their saints." She glanced at her watch. "I've got to go. Please remind Daryl about his promise." Returning the stone in its bag back to her pocket, she hopped into the driver's seat and drove off.

Hunter had an earful of food for thought. Not just about the Mojo and its power and connection to a Deity, but also about Shannon's two references to Daryl. Had she and he really become close, or was that wishful thinking on the aggressive female's part? No matter, her transferring attention to another man made him happy. The situation was improving. Maybe he'd no longer need to fear being near Shannon and the unpleasant chore of trying to tactfully fend her off.

He got into his car and sat there scratching his head. *Why did I make it a point to touch the Mojo stone? Even if Shannon's justification for its existence and spiritual transferences seem valid, they aren't in cahoots with my agnostic belief. I don't change my mind easily, either. Can a damn stone make me a believer in it, or in a Superior Being? I must be losing my mind.* He laughed aloud. *I guess true Christians, or other believers, would say I'm finding it.*

#

The chat with Shannon gave Hunter the opportunity to delay responding to Zita. He stayed out of the office all day on patrol and he did go back to the bottle trees and he talked with Daryl on the phone. He reminded Daryl about his promise to Shannon and tried to dig out the status of their relationship, but to no avail. Daryl only referred to his reassuring Shannon he didn't want any money from the record. He said it should be used to complete the museum.

That night he tuned in to Shannon's performance. She first sang *Reelin' Feelin', My Light, My Star, I'm Only Human.* Then she concluded with *Bad News Blues.* Hunter was impressed. She'd switched to the version on the record, the melodious, soulful music that resounded through the room, compelling listeners to pay attention to it. Hunter was mesmerized. She'd captured Goldie's mood precisely. He wasn't a musician, but that was clear. Shannon had music in her genes, and she'd inherited her great-grandfather's talent. Against his better judgment that it might start something, he did send Shannon an email full of compliments. It was the decent thing to do.

He was relieved that she responded in an impersonal way: *Thanks. That's high praise from a sheriff. They offered me another gig next month. I may have enough money soon to finish the museum. Shannon Brown, singer.* A Happy Face smiled up at him.

His phone rang. It was Zita. "Hunter, did you hear Shannon's concert? She's got it. Maybe even more than Goldie. What a talent. She didn't sound nervous at all, either. I'm amazed. I heard her sing before but not like this. Being on the radio brought out the best in her. Those songs and the lyrics give me goosebumps."

Hunter smiled. He knew the two were rivals over him, but he didn't take it too seriously until Zita's proposal. He found it very big of her to be so complimentary about her adversary. On the other hand, that was Zita; she wasn't petty, and she gave credit when it was due. He'd seen that in her dealings with criminals, especially teenagers. She was a fair-minded woman who reacted accordingly.

His next question was internal: *If she has such wonderful qualifications, then why don't I just say "Yes" to her proposal?* He didn't have a logical answer.

His phone rang again. "Hey, this is V. Someone left a note for you on a table in my shop. I just saw it."

"I'll be right down," Hunter replied.

V answered the door in his uniform of cut-off shorts, but this time he had on a t-shirt. He had a beer in his hand. "Want a beer, Hunter?"

"No, thanks. Who left the note?" he asked as they walked to the back of the store."

V shrugged. "You know I leave the place unlocked half the time. I went to the diner for supper and spotted it on the table when I got back. Here it is." He handed Hunter a number ten envelope with *Hunter Harley* printed in large letters.

Ripping it open, Hunter read the message: *Wait till Dewayne comes to kill you, then you'll believe in him.*

He narrowed his eyes as he inspected the envelope for clues about its sender. *And I thought the saga was over.* He knew that assumption wasn't true now. This threat was real.

"Did you see anybody when you returned home, V?" he asked without revealing the contents of the note.

"No, not that I recall. Say, is that letter bad news? No jail escapes for Dewayne or Frederica, I hope."

"Nothing I can't handle." Wishing he'd used gloves, he held the note by the corner and slipped it back in its envelope. "Let me know if you think of something. Gotta go now, I'm tired and I want to go to bed."

V nodded. "Will do."

Upstairs, Hunter took out the paper again, using gloves. V was wise. He knew he hadn't fooled him. Tomorrow, he'd check the note for fingerprints, but he didn't expect to find any. Facts kept running through his mind. Wayne was in jail. He would have been the first one notified if Wayne had escaped. How he managed to get a note delivered, Hunter couldn't fathom. There was no Dewayne. It was an empty threat, wasn't it? Uncertainty edged its way into his thoughts. He didn't want to make an issue of this, so he decided to wait it out. He went to bed with his pistol on one side and King on the other.

Feeling the need to talk to someone, he told King, "I can trust you not to blab. Hang in here with me. This has got to be the last round. I don't think there's anything to it, but I have to be on guard. Besides, in some fluke, maybe it'll lead to the urn." He patted the cat's head and it purred. "Good Boy, now let's get some sleep."

But sleep wouldn't come. Hunter's restlessness kept him awake. He flinched at any noise. He got up once when the icemaker made noise dropping ice. He spent his time trying to second guess what was going on. His analytical mind came up with a possible scenario. He knew Wayne had the Kingston gang behind him, so getting that message delivered wasn't a problem. Worse though, neither would be hiring a killer. If he was killed and the note was found, it would likely follow as proof there *was* a twin who killed Judas. Because of the way the justice system works, it could happen that it would result in a new trial for Wayne.

If I'm dead, I won't be able to do anything about it. I have to do whatever it takes to stay alive. That will take staying one step ahead of Wayne. Rest was impossible, so Hunter got out of bed and sat in his lounge chair mulling over defense mechanisms. King was in his lap snoozing. He scratched the cat's ears. "If only you could talk, I bet you could tell me the answer."

King didn't reply. Exhausted, Hunter fell asleep, but not for long. A rapping on his door soon awakened him. He looked through the peephole to see V peering in at him. So, he opened the door.

"Someone's trying to get in my place," V blurted out. "I called 911 and they're coming." His hands shook. "Come on, help me. He may have gotten inside." He paled. "Hunter this damn guy looked like Wayne, but he had a scruffy beard. I went to the trial. I know what Wayne looks like. I didn't see this man's face clearly, but I swear he, you know, he could be Dewayne. The guy may really exist." Sirens blasted out and V bolted for the elevator.

Hunter followed, distraught at his prediction coming true, except he hadn't been killed yet. Maybe it wouldn't even take a killing. Wayne would glory in the success of seeing him, the sheriff, upstaged, especially if it got him off Scot free. Hunter knew, despite logic, that could happen. The thought angered him. Judas was a criminal; his death was no loss to society; it may even be a blessing, but no one had the right to murder another person. A killer's fate should be up to a judge and a jury. Besides, as a criminal himself, Wayne deserved to be punished, not to be let off on something close to a technicality. How he'd prevent it he wasn't sure. He was positive he wasn't going to let that happen. Wayne was going to serve his time in prison.

V made his report to the police. But no evidence of a break in was resolved. As a result, it didn't cause a stir. Hunter was convinced this wasn't the end of it. Wayne was sitting on ready to pounce. The air was stirred up, leaving Hunter to wait for the other shoe to fall.

Chapter 31

A strange turn of events changed the entire situation. An unbelievable occurrence happened. Wayne had a massive stroke. He was conscious and, as a fallen-away Catholic, asked for a priest to hear his confession, a chance to make his peace with God before he died.

The priest had a vow he wouldn't break, so he couldn't reveal anything he was told under the seal of the confessional. He refused to confer with any deputies. However, he didn't have to. On his deathbed, Wayne called for Hunter and voluntarily made his own statement. He not only admitted killing Judas, but said he'd been involved in other crimes. He even listed them. He explained his reason for confessing to Hunter. "Be sure to let my son know. He's a lawyer and he knows the truth about me. He's so ashamed of me, he even changed his name." He wrote it down along with the address. "I love that boy. I don't want to die with him still hating me."

Hunter caught his breath. He recognized the name. He couldn't deliver the message. It had made the lead TV news story the day before because Wayne's son had been killed in a plane crash. He didn't let the father know his son was dead. There would be no point. *It's hard to be kind to someone like this, but I'll let him die in whatever peace he gets from thinking he's squared things with his son. It won't do any harm.*

Kingsmen gang members were brought in to pay for their crimes. They were shocked and horrified. Their leader, who pretended to be Dewayne, was Wayne, a prominent citizen of Jackson. Worse yet, he'd betrayed them and condemned them to death, or the death of living in jail, with him. None could believe their untimely fate unfolded as it did.

Neither could the citizens of Jackson who'd fallen for Dewayne's deception. All were aghast at his trickery, but more nonplussed that he'd succeeded in fooling them. But there was no denial; the facts rang true. They'd been duped and they had to admit it.

In his glory, Hunter sighed with relief. With his mind free of the threat of being murdered–Dewayne now dead, and Frederica imprisoned for life–he hoped to make a decision about where he'd go from here. It came naturally. Peace of mind consumed him when he invited Zita to dinner. Of all places, he chose the Delta Diner. Zita didn't know it, but he had Levenia close the entire place. At eight p.m. that evening, he escorted her inside. Balloons filled the entire area. White tablecloths covered the formica-topped tables. Hunter provided the fine china, crystal, and sterling silverware. A server from Jackson dressed in black and white bowed as he pulled out their chairs and dropped a white cloth napkin in their lap.

Wide-eyed Zita whispered to Hunter. "This is like being on a cruise ship. How did you arrange it? It must have cost a fortune!"

Hunter smiled back. "You're worth it, Zita."

The waiter poured Dom Perignon from the Champagne cooler filled with ice beside them and then he left.

Hunter took her hand in his. "Now it's my turn. Zita, will you marry me?"

Her own eyes full of tears, she looked into his. "Yes, you know I will." Smiling, she added, "But that's a rhetorical question; I asked you first."

While savoring the entree of Chateau Briand, Zita told him she wanted to be married in her church. They decided to have their wedding reception at the museum scheduled to open in June. "I don't know if I can wait that long," Hunter joked. "I guess I can; it's only a couple of months and I've already waited twenty years."

On a sunny Saturday, June 20, one week before the official opening of the Goldie Parsons' Museum, Zita walked down the aisle of Our Lady of Victories Catholic Church in Cleveland, Mississippi. Her father gave her away. Her mother cried throughout the entire ceremony.

Whether those were tears of joy or sorrow, no one knew. She'd said she wasn't happy that her daughter was marrying an agnostic. However, she was glad to finally have the prospect of having grandchildren.

The church was full for the old-fashioned Italian wedding. Zita wore her grandmother's dress with a long train and a veil with orange blossoms. Tippiny came from Washington to be her maid of honor. Hunter chose Chan for his best man. The men wore dark gray tuxedos. Karla, the flower girl, dressed in pink to match the maid of honor's attire, walked down the aisle smiling and tossing rose petals. Charles said he was too old to be a ring bearer. Accompanied by an organist, Shannon brought tears to some people's eyes when she sang *O Promise Me.*

The reception at the museum was attended by many of Cleveland's citizens. One person heard about the wedding but he didn't receive an invitation. Carlton came from Mobile anyway and used the opportunity to brag about his new job as a detective. His former co-workers knew he was only a file clerk but held their tongues and didn't correct him. People had to look twice to recognize V who had on a coat and a tie. Charles kept an eye on King who roamed through the crowd at will, being petted often, and making every effort to be in control.

Mama Cheche's former home was filled to capacity. It was one of Cleveland's biggest weddings. Two law enforcement officers marrying each other was a signal event. The town turned out. Shannon attended with Daryl and she didn't take her eyes off of him for one minute. If another female engaged him in conversation, Shannon grabbed his arm and guided him elsewhere. Despite their rivalry over Hunter, now that she'd made a catch of her own, she wished Shannon well. "I hope you'll have a wonderful life together," she said. Then she pulled Daryl close. "I hope we will, too." Daryl swallowed a gasp, but he couldn't free himself from her grasp.

After they cut the cake in the shape of the Bolivar sheriff's six-point star and shared a piece of it, Tippiny said, "Mama would be so pleased that you chose her house to have your wedding reception, the first event in Goldie's Museum. How proud she'd be." She looked at them out of the corner of her eye. "Hmm—she may just have arranged it herself with the mojo."

It was time to throw the bouquet. The group went outside, and Zita stood directly under the spot of the bullet hole. Turning her back, she tossed the bouquet over her shoulder. Tippiny missed it when Shannon stepped in front of her and snatched it away. "I'm going to be the next bride," she called out, holding her trophy high in the air." Casting a glance at Daryl evoked a smile from him.

Hunter and Zita wanted to be back in Cleveland for the museum's dedication six days later, so they couldn't go too far for their honeymoon. Memphis, Beale Street, and the Peabody Hotel were their destinations.

Hunter felt they were walking in the footsteps of Goldie and Eleanor Parsons and it gave him the jitters. He hoped their fate wouldn't become his and Zita's as the Mojo resurfaced. He reminded himself that it was superstition, and he didn't believe in it. But too much of it had become true for him to deny it. He'd felt a little odd recalling Zita's reply to Tippiny at the wedding reception, "I think Mama Cheche approves." Where did reality begin and end?

Regardless of Hunter's concern, he and Zita made it back in time for the Museum Dedication. It was a gala event, one that again resulted in having the entire town turn out. The streets were packed. Cars parked all over, drivers not caring if they got tickets. This was an event of a lifetime and they weren't going to miss it.

The Easter Parade was no comparison to this. Plus the local band, ten others came from Jackson and surrounding areas to participate. They'd sectioned off areas for dignitaries with raised seating so they wouldn't miss anything when the parade, led by Shannon dressed in vintage clothing dating to pre-World War II, walked by. Her nylon stockings with a seam down the back reminded older citizens of long since forgotten styles.

A huge paper-mache replica of Goldie, which only slightly resembled him, was the feature of the first float. Over sixty years had passed. Since nobody really knew exactly what he looked like, it didn't matter.

Applause from bystanders encouraged the bands to play their best. Goldie was their most famous blues singer. Who cared if the replica didn't ring true? This was a tribute to him that all were willing to observe, let the rest be hanged.

After the pomp and ceremony worthy of a king's coronation reached the Goldie Parsons' Museum, Shannon ceremoniously placed the key in the lock and turned it. The door opened revealing the artifacts testimonial to Goldie. Nobody went inside then. The graveside ceremony would be held first. Shannon took an urn filled with sawdust from a table right inside the front door. She removed Mama Cheche's Mojo stone from her beaded purse and placed it in a delicately carved box from the table, announcing, "This will be placed in a large china cabinet as soon as it's delivered. People will be able to see it. It should be on display. For now, it will be locked in a safe place." The crowd awed and ooed. All seemed to understand its significance, so they moved on.

Outside, when Shannon looked into the site where other urns were placed, she spotted an extra one. She recognized it. It was Goldie's! First, she acknowledged her discovery to Hunter. He was astounded. Then she made an announcement to the public in a gleeful voice: "Ladies and gentlemen, I have something wonderful to tell you. When they dug the hole to put a commemorative urn in the spot for Goldie's, the workmen evidently didn't know how many others were there. However, when I got ready to put in this one," she held up the substitute one, "I saw that Goldie's real urn was already in its place." She smiled. "So we now have to fill that extra spot." Applause and expressions of wonder filled the air.

Hunter stood mesmerized. All he could think of was that Frederica had mocked him by placing the missing urn in plain sight. How she did it befuddled him. Amazing! This was Mama Cheche's house. Goldie's last moments were spent there before he walked to the Sunflower River and perished. Mama Cheche also had the same fate. With no reason to voice those remembrances, he remained silent. After so long a time, the last nail was in the coffin. All could have closure.

Hunter didn't hear what the other speakers said. His mind was on all of the activities of the past few weeks. So much had transpired, the notes in the bottle trees, Daryl's connection to Goldie, now finding the urn, but mainly the craziness with Frederica and Dewayne, not to mention the bizarre deathbed admission of Wayne Kingston. Deathbed confessions weren't unheard of, but they were rare. Who'd ever believe a gang leader like Kingston would succumb to such a thing?

But who'd believe a hard-nosed sheriff would end up–what? He married in the Catholic Church, but did he believe in God? Since Hunter didn't know, how could anyone else? No matter, marriage was sacred to him. He'd kept his vow in his first marriage long after no marriage existed; he'd keep it in this one: *Till death do us part.*

Epilogue

When things settled down, Shannon honed her musical talent by writing a song. One night after closing time, she went to the museum. She sat alone in front of an enlarged wedding photo of Goldie and Eleanor that she'd had restored and enlarged done in oil. Underneath it, the Mojo stone rested on a silver tray in a glass case.

With only a lamp illuminating the room, shadows on the wall took on forms. Was Goldie there leading her? Remembering his song *Bad News Blues*, an eerie feeling crept over her. His influence seemed to permeate her very being. She typed words on a laptop as lyrics and the title *C'est Fini* came from nowhere. With a talent she'd inherited, she strummed on her guitar and a tune evolved. Inspiration filled her soul as past events surfaced. So did the blues as she blurted out these lyrics:

C'est Fini

All my sorrows and miseries

Chased me down relentlessly,

Never thought I'd find release.
C'est fini.

Life pursued me all up and down.
I was lost but now I'm found.
No more troubled by what I've seen.
C'est fini.

I was followed by the blues
Couldn't tell what's false or true.
Didn't know what I could do,
Locked in a jail of history.

I was haunted by the past
Hopes and dreams were sinking fast,
But I've found my path at last.
Turns out, my heart held the key.

Now it's over
I'm on my way
My tomorrows start here today.
From now on I'm truly free
C'est Fini.

Did she still have to live out her legacy? Was the trauma over, or would her legacy still continue? She laid her guitar at her feet and stared into the glass case: "Mojo stone, you know; you tell me!"

She blinked and a picture of Arcachon, a beach town in the South of France, formed in her mind. She was thrilled to have a singing engagement there in June and was taking French lessons because she, Charles, and Karla would stay for the summer and go to Paris. C'est Fini was more than the title she chose for her song; it was her statement of confidence. Everything was looking up.

Shannon's spirits soared. *I'm getting the best of both worlds—Goldie's talent but not his fate. I'm a star, not a very big one, but important enough to be invited to perform in another country. Hooray.* She looked at the Mojo stone which seemed to shine brighter. *You gave me my answer, and it's a positive one. Goldie's song to his wife, 'My Light, My Star,' rings true.* She pointed to the stone. *When I leave for France, you'll be in my pocket.* Beaming a smile, Shannon turned out the light and left Goldie's Museum content that her future was bright.

C'est fini.

Melody of Malice

About the Authors

Mary S. Palmer has a BA (Cum Laude) in English from the University of South Alabama. Her Master's Degree is also in English with a Concentration in Creative Writing. She teaches English at Faulkner University and has been a member of the adjunct faculty at Huntingdon College. A native of Mobile, Alabama, she taught at Faulkner State Community College in Fairhope, Alabama many years.

She has published twenty books, three plays, and numerous poems. *Boyington Oak: A Grave Injustice* was released in November 2019; *Tourism Writing – A New Literary Genre Unveiling the History, Mystery, and Economy of Places and Events*, was written with a grant from Faulkner University.

Palmer's short story *The Concrete Block Wall* won the Hackney Award in 2016. That story is featured in her book *Commas for Soul Searchers*. She loves to travel and uses those experiences in her writings.

Paula Lenor Webb, has a Master's in Library and Information Science from the University of Alabama. She is currently a tenured Librarian at the University of South Alabama, in Mobile. Ms. Webb has always enjoyed research and documented her local history findings in her first book, *Mobile Under Siege: Surviving the Union Blockade*, in 2016. She has continued pursuing this avenue of research with her latest book, *Such a Woman: The Life of Octavia Walton LeVert*. Mississippi Mojo… and Murder is her first fiction book.